An Unforgettable Stranger

Robyn C Rye

Published by robyncrye, 2023.

Table of Contents

Author's message

As a reader, you may wonder why some words seem misspelt, but as an Australian writer, I use English spellings rather than American ones. So, NO! I am not a poor speller, and I have used the spell check, but with an Australian slant.

Thank you for joining me in telling the story of Shannon and Jax. I hope you enjoyed their story as much as I enjoyed recounting it.

If you enjoyed the book and have a moment to spare, I would appreciate a brief review on the page or site where you purchased the book. Reviews from readers like you make a massive difference in helping new readers find stories like An Unforgettable Stranger. Your help in spreading the word is appreciated.

Thank you!

Contact me at

robyncrye.author@gmail.com

Prologue

Shannon entered the town centre and pulled into a parking space to reload the map on her phone. She had the directions to the house, but preferred that the woman on her app give her the instructions. Bubbling with excitement, Shannon fumbled while typing the street address and had to calm herself with a few deep breaths. Once she sorted the address, Shannon pulled away from the park and headed to the small suburb of Colston. Today was the first day of the rest of her life. That's how the saying goes, but it felt like the correct description in her case. After years of studying hard, she secured a partial scholarship to the University of Westmead to pursue a degree in Physiotherapy. Small suburbs sprang up around the town to accommodate students, and Shannon headed to her new shared house today. She hadn't met her new housemates, and despite her sister's warnings about thieving housemates and slovenly behaviour, Shannon was excited to meet the girls who would share her home. After following the lady on Google, Shannon arrived at a neat brick veneer house. A car sat under the carport, so Shannon guessed at least one of her housemates was there.

Shannon drove her car into the driveway but angled it to the side so that her housemate could move the other car. Once she removed her suitcase, Shannon pulled it along the cracked walkway until she reached the front door. The bell rang loudly, and then the door opened. A blond-haired woman about Shannon's size opened the door. Her friendly smile welcomed Shannon, and her spirits rose.

"Hi, I'm Shannon."

"Hi, Shannon; I'm Amelia. Please bring your gear in, and then we can discuss it. I am unsure when Beck will arrive or if Beck is a boy or a girl, but I guess we must wait and see."

As Amelia gave Shannon the tour of the house, Shannon could see that Amelia had placed her luggage in the largest of the bedrooms.

"So, first in best dressed?"

Amelia grinned. "Yep, that's how it works, so if you're smart, you'll put your luggage in the room across the hall because the third bedroom is smaller."

Shannon dragged her suitcase into the bedroom Amelia suggested, then returned to the car to carry in boxes and another case. By the time she had sorted her room, the sun had begun to sink, and the girls decided to buy takeout for dinner. After determining their preferences, Amelia called the pizza shop to place a delivery order.

"How long have you been in Colston?"

"I arrived two days ago and met with the real estate agent the next day. She gave me the keys, the garbage and mail schedule, and a stern warning about not partying and disturbing the neighbours."

The clanging of the doorbell interrupted the conversation, and Amelia and Shannon went to open the door. A delivery boy and a woman stood on the doorstep. The woman had vibrant red hair, and her short stature did not diminish her bubbly personality in the least. Amidst greetings and introductions, the girls headed for the kitchen.

"Yum, pizza. Are we going to spend the next four years eating takeout?"

"No, but we were waiting for you to arrive and decided on dinner. Join us, and then we can help you bring your gear in from your car."

"There is no car, and unless the neighbours are honest, I need to bring my luggage in now because the taxi driver refused to carry it any further than the driveway."

The girls followed Beck outside, grabbed boxes and bags, and carried them inside.

"Sorry, last in gets the worst room."

Beck shrugged. "I only intend to sleep there, so it doesn't matter. Can we eat and then work out the logistics of sharing a house?"

As the weeks passed, the girls became better acquainted. Sharing with two other people had its downside. Still, on the plus side, someone was usually around to chat with, celebrate academic achievements, or commiserate over less-than-stellar results. Beck and Amelia were more sociable than Shannon, who rarely lifted her head from her books. With only a partial scholarship, she had to receive high grades to secure financial assistance for the second half of her course. Beck and Amelia juggled part-time jobs at the fast food restaurant in the town, but with upcoming placements and a heavy volume of work, Shannon couldn't schedule a part-time job amongst her other commitments.

With the first year of her course drawing to a close, Shannon was excited to return home to see her family. Although Colston was only three hours away, her family and she never seemed to find a time that suited them, so they kept in touch by phone and text and left the visiting until the holidays. Shannon felt a twinge of guilt; now was the time of year when businesses were looking for casual workers, and she could build up her bank account if she worked through the holidays. However, the draw of going home was strong, so she resisted. There would be enough time to take a job next year when she sorted out her classes and placements. Beck and Amelia were staying in Colston for the holidays, so Shannon felt it was safe to leave most of her possessions and take only the essentials home. With a cheery wave, she left her housemates and drove toward home.

Chapter One

One year later

Shannon groaned; her feet ached, and she felt hot and sweaty. Working in a fast-food restaurant was no walk in the park, and she regretted her decision to stay in Colston during the holidays to earn some money to tide her over for the coming semester. One positive aspect Shannon enjoyed was chatting with some regular customers. Recently, a male customer would join her line whenever he visited the store, and on a few occasions, when there was a backlog of orders, he would chat with Shannon while waiting. Shannon looked forward to seeing the guy who had introduced himself as Andrew. Unlike many of the men on campus, Andrew wasn't cocky and full of himself, and even though he was a good-looking man, he never put on airs or talked down to Shannon.

One afternoon, as she took a break, Andrew approached and asked if he could join her; Shannon was happy for his company. Andrew fidgeted with his napkin when her break ran out and said, "Can I take you out for a meal during the week? I'm not financial enough for a fancy restaurant, but I can do better than McDonald's."

Shannon laughed at his quip but quickly accepted his invitation.

The meal they shared on Thursday night was the beginning of Shannon's first serious relationship. She and Andrew spent their spare time together, and even though Shannon still had to study and complete hospital placements for her course, the two were a common sight around campus.

The downside to her relationship was that Amelia and Andrew didn't get on. Given how much time she spent with him, the antagonism between her best friend and her boyfriend was uncomfortable. Shannon wondered if Amelia was jealous, but her friend wouldn't say what her problem was. The discord between two of her favourite people caused Shannon strain, and, with the need to concentrate on her studies, she decided to set aside time alone each week with Andrew and her girlfriends. Shannon's night out with her friends caused a rift between Shannon and Andrew. Andrew wasn't happy that Shannon and her friends were going to the local drinking spot most students preferred, but having already decided that she wanted to keep her boyfriend and best friend happy, Shannon shrugged off his concern. Her boyfriend dominated most of her spare time, and a night out with her girlfriends shouldn't concern him.

The girls decided that, so no one had to be the designated driver, they would order an Uber when they were ready to go home. As the drinks flowed, the girls chatted, danced and gossiped. Shannon felt more relaxed than she had for ages, with no thoughts of assignments and work commitments plaguing her. When Amelia, who faced the door, stiffened, Shannon glanced over her shoulder to see the problem. Andrew stood inside the door, scanning the crowd. When his eyes landed on her, Andrew navigated the dancing patrons and walked up to her table. Not happy to see him when it had taken lots of altering schedules to make time for her friends to meet, she raised her eyebrow in enquiry.

"Andrew, what are you doing here?"

Andrew flashed her what he hoped was a winning smile and said, "I know you have to work tomorrow, so I thought I'd save you the cost of an Uber."

Shannon shook her head. "Thanks for the thought, but we aren't ready to leave yet."

Andrew grinned. "I missed you tonight, sweetheart. I'll wait for you and drive you home when you're ready."

Amelia entered the conversation.

"Andrew, buzz off. Can't you let Shannon spend time with her female friends instead of expecting her to devote all her free time to you?"

When Andrew opened his mouth to respond, Shannon knew this disagreement would soon become a slanging match. Anxious to keep the peace, she rose from her table. After collecting her bag and sculling the last drink, she turned to her friends and shrugged in apology. Grabbing Andrew's arm, she said, "Let's go."

As Andrew drove, Shannon sat quietly, unwilling to talk to Andrew until they stopped and he had no distractions.

"Why did you come to the pub tonight? Did you think I was hitting on single blokes? Did you think I would fall drunk and be a target for men with bad intentions?"

"I told you, I came because I knew you had to work tomorrow and didn't want you to go to work with a hangover. Besides, I miss you when you're not around."

"I wasn't going to get drunk, and my friends were there to look after me. It took ages for us to align our schedules, and then you swoop in and tell me it's bedtime as though I'm ten years old. I don't particularly appreciate your interference, Andrew."

When Shannon alighted from the car, Andrew didn't speak, and as soon as she closed the door, he sped off. Shannon momentarily considered calling an Uber and returning to the pub, but she decided she didn't want to ruin anyone else's night with her bad mood. The sound of a car pulling up out front and closing doors drew Shannon to the window. Her friends walked to the front door, and when she opened it, she discovered they had brought the pub to her. Her friends held bottles of alcohol and nibbles, and the tangy smell of pizza and chips wafted through the air. Shannon laughed, and Amelia high-fived her.

"If the kill-joy boyfriend thinks you should be home, we decided to bring the fun to you. Why do you put up with that douche? He is too needy and controlling, and if you're not careful, he will control more and more of your life until the Shannon we know disappears."

As the girls drank and ate, Shannon considered Amelia's comments. Was she right? Was Andrew intent on controlling her? Perhaps if she expressed her concerns, he would reconsider his behaviour. Shannon liked Andrew a lot; he was considerate and protective when he wasn't bossy. Shannon liked that part of him, but didn't like it when he inserted himself into her friendships.

Chapter Two

Two Years later

With the problems that arose during wedding planning, Shannon wondered if she would ever reach the point of walking down the aisle. Some difficulties arose around food; Andrew's sister was a vegan and wanted a special menu for herself and other vegans. Shannon was happy to ask the caterers to prepare a special meal, but since there were no other vegans among the guests, she had no intention of wasting money on food that would go uneaten. Andrew wanted a buffet meal, but Kathy Wetcott pointed out that the cost was exorbitant because people serving themselves often loaded their plates excessively, even if they couldn't eat it all. She compromised on the buffet by hiring servers, and so it went with disagreements on the cake, the wedding favours and the colour theme.

The suits Andrew favoured for his groomsmen made Shannon cringe, and when she tried to convince him that more conservative suits would be better than the electric blue suits he chose, he replied that he wouldn't interfere with her bridesmaids' dresses, so she had no say on the suits. It seemed that the wedding was to be one compromise after another. Shannon gave way and let Andrew have his way wherever possible, but there was one issue: she refused to let him have his way. Andrew wanted Shannon to use his sister and cousin as her attendants, but Shannon wanted Amelia and Beck. At the beginning of the conversation about attendants, Andrew tried cajoling, pointing out that his choices were family, and she should use them. When Shannon refused to concede, he bullied her, trying to change her mind. Shannon lost her temper as the argument raged in the Westcotts' kitchen.

"Damn you, Andrew, this is my wedding, too. I have compromised on food, favours, colour theme and the cake. You have chosen suits I hate, and if our marriage is going to be a life of me compromising to keep you happy, I'm not sure I want to proceed. My friends are my attendants at the wedding preparation, and our engagement is over. Decide how many relatives you'd like to have as my attendants, because if you have to have everything your way, I suggest you find another bride. Please leave my parents' house while you consider your decision. I'm done with compromising."

The slam of the front door echoed in the silent kitchen. With a shuddering breath, Shannon looked at her mother.

"Am I being unreasonable? I know he doesn't like Amelia, but with a sister of my own and my friends to help, I don't want people I barely know as my attendants."

Before her mum could answer, her dad barrelled into the kitchen.

"What the dickens is wrong with Longley? He lit out of here like the devil was after him."

Kathy Westcott patted her husband's arm.

"Let's sit down, and I'll put the kettle on. We need to discuss this last snag and find a solution."

Once the kitchen's occupants had a mug of tea, Kathy said, "Shannon, do you want to tell your dad what happened?"

Shannon relayed the gist of the argument, and her father frowned.

"I thought it was brides they called bridezillas when they caused problems, but it seems your intended is a groomzilla. What are you going to do?"

"Dad, I have compromised on the food, the favours, the colour theme and the cake, but I refuse to have his sister and cousin as my attendants. I want Amelia, Beck and Camille as my attendants, and if he refuses to concede this time, there will be no wedding."

"Is that a bit drastic?"

"Dad, if he can't compromise on this, after all the concessions I have made, we have no hope of a happy marriage. Maybe we are not meant to be. The ball is in his court now, so I must wait for him to call me."

Kathy Westcott frowned. "You don't seem too upset with the possibility of cancelling your wedding."

"I'm too angry to be upset at the moment. Andrew's changes have exhausted me, and if he refuses my request, this whole ordeal will be over. When Camille's ready to marry, tell her to elope."

Shannon heard nothing from Andrew for the best part of a week, although his mother did ring, attempting to convince Shannon to use Andrew's sister and cousin as her attendants. Shannon had always had cordial relations with her prospective in-laws, but the thought that they would try to coerce her to comply with Andrew's wishes infuriated her. Shannon wanted Andrew's mother to know what had happened before her stipulation, so she divulged all that had occurred in her attempts to organise the wedding.

"Mrs Longley, I resent that you would choose to interfere in this argument between Andrew and me because you don't know what has gone before. Did Andrew bother to tell you that I wanted a sit-down meal, and he wanted a buffet? I compromised, and we are having servers dish the food at the buffet instead of my parents paying a fortune for wasted food. I have compromised on the colour theme, the wedding favours and the cake. To add insult to injury, your son has chosen electric blue suits for himself and the groomsmen, ignoring my concerns and the need to change the colour of my bridesmaid dresses. When I walk down the aisle, the wedding I dreamed of will not be what I get, and I refuse to compromise further. I won't walk down the aisle if the attendants are not my choice. The ball is in Andrew's court, but he had better decide soon, or otherwise, I will cancel the arrangements Mum and I have made."

"Oh, my goodness. I apologise for my interference when I didn't know the changes you have made to what we hope will be your only wedding. I know Andrew can be pushy, but to have your choices disregarded is concerning. With luck, I can encourage Andrew to change his mind."

Shannon waited two more days before she received a phone call from Andrew. The gist of the call was that he wanted to meet her, and they agreed on a time and a place. Mrs Westcott voiced her concern about meeting Andrew in a public place, but Shannon thought that he had chosen the pub so that she couldn't make a fuss if she didn't like what he had to say. Despite her anger at Andrew's high-handedness over the wedding arrangements, Shannon still loved the man when he was reasonable and hoped they could resolve their issues.

As Shannon waited, she questioned the sense of having a personal discussion in the almost deserted coffee shop. A packed bar would surely be better if Andrew wanted a public place. Here, the patrons would be privy to everything the couple said. Shannon shrugged; it seemed they couldn't even agree on a venue for a meaningful discussion. When Andrew entered the shop, Shannon waited for him to approach, but he delayed their meeting by stopping by the counter. With his drink in hand, he approached the table, and his lack of manners in not ordering her a drink angered Shannon. Once Andrew arrived, Shannon let him make the opening statements and see where the conversation went.

"Shannon, my mother talked to me about the changes I wanted you to make to the wedding plans, and she pointed out that a wedding is for the bride, and the groom just gets to be along on the ride. She said it was okay for me to choose the suits, but they had to be both conservative and tasteful, a standard she doubted my opinion could meet. My mother also said that it was acceptable for the groom to help choose the wedding cake's flavour and to have a view on the type of meal served, but after that, I should butt out. She thought my desire to disregard your choices in favour of mine was selfish and unreasonable, and she said if you called the whole thing off, she wouldn't blame you."

"Now I know what your mother thinks, but what about you? And where do we go from here?"

Andrew rubbed a hand over his hair and looked down at his coffee. Shannon tensed, expecting the breakup to come any minute.

"I'm sorry for overruling your choices. I wanted the wedding to be perfect, but my idea of perfection differed from yours. I had no right to interfere in your selection of colours, favours, flowers, or so much more. My choice of suits was unwise, and I hope we can rectify the changes you made to appease me."

"And what of my attendants?"

Andrew looked pained but said, "They are your attendants, so you should choose. I still believe you should use family, but if you decide not to, that is your decision."

"Where do we go from here?"

"I will leave you to the alteration of the arrangements, and while you do that, I will visit the hire shop and choose more conservative attire."

Chapter Three

As Amelia fussed with her veil, Shannon sighed. At one point in time, Shannon thought this day would never come. After Andrew's capitulation, Shannon had changed the arrangements to suit her, and now she had the wedding she wanted. Andrew's chosen suits were both elegant and conservative and would look fabulous in the photos paired with her attendants in their rose-coloured dresses.

When her father arrived, Amelia whispered, 'It's not too late to back out." And Shannon swatted her friend on the arm.

"No backing out, just moving forward."

Her attendants gathered their posies, and Shannon hooked her arm through her father's. He patted her hand, and then they were on their way.

The wedding and the reception were a blur to Shannon. The day flew past, and after the good wishes of friends and family, she and Andrew headed for the motel her new husband had chosen for the night. Tomorrow, they would fly to Gardner Island and the resort there. Andrew had spared no expense; the week away would let them both de-stress. Shannon knew the calm and luxury the resort offered were a break from the reality they would face when they returned home, but she intended to enjoy it for now.

The resort offered many activities, and while Shannon knew she and her new husband couldn't restrict themselves to the bedroom, she did wish Andrew hadn't signed them up for so many. Andrew's lack of interest in spending time in the bedroom concerned Shannon, and she hoped their very different libidos didn't cause problems in the future.

When she expressed her concern, Andrew laughed and said they had a lifetime for bedroom activities, but this might be their only chance at experiencing all the resort had to offer.

Their week away passed too quickly, and Shannon grimaced at the unpacking that she had to do. Andrew had left her to unpack both cases as he was due at work tomorrow and had emails and phone calls to catch up on. Finding a space for her belongings took a while because Andrew's flat was relatively spacious, but it lacked many cupboards, apart from those in the kitchen. Sorting clean and dirty clothes as she unpacked, Shannon decided that while the holiday had been terrific, unpacking clothes covered in sand was not an experience she enjoyed. Knowing that she would have other items to unpack besides her suitcase, Shannon took eight days' leave, and her return to work was not due for another three days.

With Andrew's attention focused on work, Shannon dealt with the mundane tasks that came with her relocation. A glance in the fridge revealed a shrivelled-up carrot and a juice carton. Neither item would contribute to making an evening meal, and Shannon debated whether to go to the supermarket or finish unpacking. She decided the unpacking could wait, but the food would not, so she left a note for Andrew and headed to the shops. As she wandered through the supermarket, the trolley's contents grew, and at last, she decided that she had more than enough. Shannon enjoyed baking, and her cookies were famous amongst their family, so she bought cooking supplies and meal ingredients.

When Andrew finally emerged from his office, he raised his eyebrows and surveyed the shopping bags on the kitchen counter.

"Good grief! Did someone tell you there would be a food shortage, and you decided to stock up?"

"Funny, man. Shopping once a week rather than buying bits and pieces every night is much more efficient. Besides, I'm not too fond of shopping, so it's best to do it once, and I don't have to think about it for a while. And I guess you don't want to order takeout every night?"

"Okay, whatever you think. After I finished with the emails and phone calls, I worked out a five-year financial plan for us, and after dinner, I want to show it to you and get your feedback."

"The plan is for five years?"

"Yes, I think it's best to plan and know where we are going."

"Okay, I'm game. Tell me what you planned."

Andrew placed a sheet of paper in front of Shannon.

"We need to sort out how much we put into a joint account, and because I earn more than you, we will work it out as a percentage of our wages. The remainder of our money will be deposited into individual accounts. I propose that for the first two years, we both concentrate on our careers. If we save most of our money by the second year, we will have enough funds to buy two family-type cars. Once we've purchased new vehicles, we will have another year or two to get together enough money for a deposit on a family home. If we make fortnightly payments instead of monthly, we can pay off the loan faster. Another tactic to pay off the loan is to increase the charges, even by fifty or a hundred dollars a fortnight. What do you think so far?"

Shannon drew a deep breath. "It all sounds reasonable, but when do we plan on having children? Is that in your plan?"

"Yes, we can discuss when we want children on our fifth anniversary. Because having children will affect you more, you can make informed decisions about what you want to do. If you wish to return to work full-time, we'll be able to afford child care, but you can choose a part-time job or stay at home, whichever you prefer."

"And what of incidental spending and holidays?"

"We'll need to keep our incidental spending to a minimum and take only a portion of our holidays to bank time and income against the time you take off work."

"It seems like you have thought of everything. I don't have any objections to the plan, but the best thing about a goal is that it is flexible enough to meet the changed circumstances."

"You're right, but God willing, things will go according to plan."

17

Chapter Four

Andrew and Shannon settled into a routine that included lunch at his parents' place on a Sunday and a meal with Shannon's parents on Wednesday nights. Shannon discovered that Andrew rarely visited her on Saturday afternoons during their courtship because he and his friends would often watch football. The men didn't invite wives and girlfriends. Sometimes, the men watched football at the stadium, while others watched it at someone's home. The men rotated venues, and the afternoons were filled with beer and takeout. Shannon was not so insecure that she resented the time Andrew spent with his mates, but his constant harping about incidental spending chafed when she knew how much he spent each Saturday.

Shannon wished that Amelia and Bree lived closer so that she could spend time with them, but a four-hour drive for a visit and then a return trip were too much. As the football season wound to a close, Shannon hoped Andrew might consider taking some weekend trips, but he dashed her hopes when the men swapped from football to cricket.

It became clear to Shannon that she had to find some hobbies or activities. The perfect opportunity arose when she heard some colleagues planning to meet up for a run on Saturday. Shannon declined when Dinah asked if she wanted to join them; running was not her thing. Dinah explained that a group of colleagues joined a parkrun, and sprinting, jogging, walking, or a combination of those paces was acceptable. Shannon was not usually shy, but finishing the five kilometres last was daunting. She expressed her concern, and

Natalie, another of the Parkrunners, said, "You will never be last. We have a tail walker whose job is to be last. Everyone gets an individual time slot, and you can volunteer if you attend regularly. We sit around for ages afterwards, fixing the world, drinking coffee and gossiping. Try it out; I don't think you will regret becoming involved."

And so, Shannon's Saturdays became more exciting and more fun. She tried to explain to Andrew what she had done, but he showed little interest, so Shannon decided to keep her walks and the people she met private.

As they approached their second anniversary, Shannon read reviews and checked the price and safety ratings of the type of cars that interested her. With so many cars available, she and Andrew needed to discuss buying the two vehicles. While Andrew favoured the big SUVs, Shannon wanted a smaller vehicle; she wasn't opposed to a smaller SUV but didn't want to be one of the drivers she often saw struggling to park the behemoth vehicles. Before Andrew left for work, Shannon broached the subject of the cars.

"Can we do this tonight when I get home? I have an early meeting and will be late if I don't leave now."

Andrew kissed Shannon on the cheek and headed out the door. With her departure time looming, Shannon had no option but to leave the subject with her now-absent husband until after work. When Shannon arrived at work, she discovered she was the only physio on duty because many staff members were ill so today would be extra busy. The day flew past, and Shannon slumped in the staffroom, attempting to get up the energy to drive home. Takeout tonight might be the way to go because Shannon doubted she had the energy to make a meal. She could discuss car options with Andrew as they ate rather than wait for ages while she prepared a meal.

Andrew arrived home looking hassled and angry, and Shannon's spirits dimmed at the thought of discussing anything with her husband tonight. When he came home in a lousy mood, Shannon knew he would pick at her most of the evening until one or the other retired to bed. Shannon poured her husband a drink, and he slumped in the kitchen chair.

"Why have you not prepared a meal? Am I to go hungry tonight while you follow some bizarre diet?"

"You know full well that I don't diet, but today was extra busy, and I'm too tired to prepare a meal. Our takeout will be here soon."

"If you continue to spend money will-nilly, our financial plan will never work."

"Andrew, the financial plan is not ours; it is yours, and it doesn't seem to stop you from meeting your mates and splurging on beer and pizza. This meal is the first I've ordered in over six months, so my incidental spending is nowhere near your level. If you are so worried, why don't I retire to the lounge room with a drink while you prepare a meal?"

Andrew scowled at Shannon and stomped away from the table. She knew she shouldn't react to his barbs, but why should she be the only one in the household responsible for providing the food? Andrew rarely helped around the house; his one big sacrifice was mowing the lawn on Sunday, and even that task might disappear soon, as he was investigating the cost of hiring a mowing contractor.

The beer and the Chinese takeaway had dimmed Andrew's poor attitude, and when he raised the subject of the cars, Shannon collected the paperwork she had on each of the preferred brands and types. Andrew flipped through the documents and said, "I like the bigger SUV that Nissan has. What is your preference?"

"I thought you might go that way. If I buy the smaller vehicle or even a sedan, we might be able to get a discount."

"Okay, we'll do that."

" It is our anniversary; I would like to go out for a meal. I don't generally mind cooking for us, but I would like someone to make me a meal on a special occasion."

Andrew nodded. "I will tell Mum to whip up something fancy for lunch on Sunday."

"You know that is not what I mean. I want us to have a meal together at a nice restaurant."

"Who is paying for this nice meal?"

"We have a joint account that I am confident can stretch to paying for a meal."

"No, we aren't spending money on things we don't need. You....."

The ringing of Andrew's phone cut off his conversation, and Shannon looked aghast as he answered the phone before they finished their conversation. Why would Andrew take a call and ignore what she had to say? From the conversation she could hear, Andrew's boss wanted him to do something work-related now, and damn him, he agreed.

"Yes, yes, I can get right on that."

When he ended the call, Shannon glared at him. "We haven't finished what we were talking about."

"Yes, we have, and I have work to do, so I'm not spending endless hours with you arguing a point."

Shannon sighed. The next three years stretched endlessly ahead. Would Andrew tighten the purse strings or loosen them when the fifth anniversary came around? Agreeing to his plan when they first married now seemed a monumental mistake. Because Andrew earned more than she did, he felt comfortable spending money on incidentals while forbidding her to do the same. Shannon gave up trying to discuss the issue with her husband when she saw him take his laptop out of its case and begin typing. She had lost him for the night, so she reached for a book and headed to the bedroom. Three hours later, while Andrew continued typing frantically, Shannon turned out the light and closed her eyes, willing herself to sleep.

Chapter Five

Shannon survived Andrew's penny-pinching ways, and much to her surprise, they had weathered the years that Andrew had identified in his financial plan. With twelve months left, Shannon wanted the time to swiftly pass so that she could join Amelia on a shopping spree. Over the past four years, she had bought no new clothes or shoes and spent little on beauty care and haircuts, and the last twelve months couldn't go fast enough.

Andrew was excited and eager to discuss a tremendous new opportunity with Shannon when he came home that night.

"Mr Simms has asked me to take on more responsibility to ease the workload on some of the other consultants. It would mean more hours, but he said it would look good on my next promotion application. The extra time will affect you because I will have less time to spend with you, but it should be worth the effort in the long run."

"Will your Mr Simms pay you more? Why doesn't he hire more staff if there is more work for the consultants? Asking staff to sacrifice their time to make him rich is not right. Who are the overworked consultants, and when you take some of their work, will it mean that when they go home, you will still be slogging away?"

"For goodness' sake, can't you see the opportunity here?"

"No, I can only see the downside. You've worked for the company for more than five years; in that time, they have promoted staff to supervisors and assistant managers, and you've never got a look-in. And if your Mr Simms was going to promote you, don't you think it is overdue? I think it is time for you to start exploring other job opportunities. Loyalty is fine if reciprocated, but from my perspective, it is not."

"Well, that's too bad because I already accepted."

"Then what was the point in talking to me about it?"

"I thought you'd be supportive. I guess I was wrong."

"Since we are having a heart-to-heart, I need to say something that will probably make you angry, but I refuse to live like your housekeeper any longer without voicing my unhappiness."

"What rubbish is this? My housekeeper, what is that supposed to mean?"

"For years, we have had sex, missionary-style, in bed on a Sunday night. I knew after our honeymoon that you and I weren't a good match in the bedroom, but I hoped I could loosen you up and make our sex life more frequent and enjoyable. Whenever I tried to initiate a sexual encounter, you said you were tired or had to get up early. Your lack of physical response makes me feel ugly and unattractive. You've been pushing me away for years, and I want to know why. Do you not fancy me? Is there something medically wrong with you?"

Shannon watched her husband's response, wary of his reaction to her criticism.

"Normal people don't fuck like rabbits. There is nothing wrong with me, although I think something might be wrong with you. What do they call oversexed women? Nymphomaniacs, is that the word?"

Shannon felt like Andrew had slapped her. She had tried to talk about something that had troubled her for the last four years, and he resorted to insults. Rising from her seat, Shannon walked towards her bedroom; she felt defeated and wondered what the point of remaining married was when the life she wanted was now tainted with his criticism.

"Are you going to make dinner?"

Shannon snorted. "Ask the housekeeper; she might rustle up something for you."

That night, Shannon slept in the guest room; she was not sharing a bed with a man who had accused her of being a nymphomaniac. She wasn't sure where she went from here, but Shannon knew that Andrew had a long road to travel before she shared his bed.

Shannon wanted to talk to Amelia, but her best friend's dislike of Andrew might mean her advice wasn't impartial. Moving like a zombie, Shannon went to work and came home again each day, hoping for an improvement in her relationship. True to his word, Andrew took on more work and often arrived home at eight or nine o'clock. Shannon left his meal in the warming drawer, so it dried out and was barely edible when he came home. Often in the morning, she found his dinner in the bin, so he had eaten before returning home.

Andrew's financial plan was working perfectly as their marriage splintered apart. The more Andrew worked, the less time he spent at home, and Shannon became lonely. She accepted her workmates' invitation to join them for a meal and a drink on a Thursday night. Andrew never arrived in time for dinner with her parents, and she opted out of Sunday lunches with his family, not wanting to attend alone. Shannon joined a group on Monday night that practised Karate, looking for a distraction from her damaged marriage. While she had no desire to excel in the discipline, she enjoyed the physical activity, which left her relaxed and helped her sleep more peacefully.

After six months of living solitary lives, Andrew came home early one night, and when Shannon arrived, his packed suitcase was standing at the front door. Shannon left her bag on the kitchen counter and walked through the house to Andrew's study.

"What is the bag packed for? Where are you going?"

"Mr Simms wants me to attend a conference in Longpine. It's another step towards my promotion."

Shannon wanted to scoff, but controlled the urge and said,

"How long will you be gone?"

"For a week, there are business meetings after the conference finishes."

"Well, I hope you achieve all you set out to."

"I'll do what I have to do to gain the promotion I deserve. Things will be better when that happens."

Shannon nodded and walked away; she didn't believe the issues tearing their marriage apart would ever improve. His delusion that more money would improve the situation proved how far off track they had gone. With their fifth anniversary approaching, Shannon wondered if they could put the hurt behind them and repair their marriage, or was it mortally wounded?

Chapter Six

After he attended the conference, Andrew's late nights continued. Shannon couldn't decide if her husband wanted to add a few more zeros to his bank account or if he was having an affair. The latter thought almost beggared belief; the man couldn't bed his wife, so how would he get the energy to bed another woman? When she and Andrew first began dating, his possessiveness nearly drove Shannon mad, but that behaviour changed when they married. If Andrew loved her, and he said he did, why was bedding his wife such an unpleasant task? Was their lack of sex life because Andrew loved her like a sister, not a wife, which made bedding her an unpleasant task? She and Andrew had barely spoken to each other since her attempt at discovering why their sex life was so disappointing, but tonight, she wanted him to come home for tea. Shannon rose early enough to catch Andrew before he left for work. As she sipped her coffee, she waited for her husband to enter the kitchen. He eyed her warily when he entered and muttered "Good morning" as he collected his coffee.

"Andrew, today is our fifth wedding anniversary, and we must discuss where we go. Could you please arrive in time for dinner tonight?"

Andrew shrugged. "I'll see what I can do."

Shannon was on tenterhooks all day, wondering if tonight would mark the end of her marriage or if Andrew was willing to attend counselling to help repair the damage to their union. Tonight, they wouldn't discuss having children unless Andrew agreed to changes in how he approached their marriage. Shannon zipped around the shops to purchase a few ingredients to make Andrew's favourite dish. Once she had prepared the meal, she set the table with the cutlery and dinner set her mother had gifted her, which she kept for best. After checking the meal's progress, Shannon showered and, from the back of her cupboard, found a dress she hadn't worn since the early days of her marriage. As Andrew's arrival time approached, Shannon removed the meat from the oven and allowed it a few minutes to rest.

With her eye on the clock, Shannon paced. The meat had sat on the bench for too long, and the excellent cut of beef was drying out quickly. When Shannon rang Andrew's phone, it went to voicemail. Shannon was unprepared to wait longer, so she served her dinner and forced herself to eat. At nine o'clock, Shannon cleared the table and put the leftovers in the refrigerator after dishing a meal for Andrew. She left the meal on the table and went to prepare for bed. Andrew's absence answered the question Shannon had tortured herself with all day; the answer was obvious: their marriage was over. Shannon sat in a recliner, waiting for her husband to arrive. At eleven o'clock, she heard his car pull into the driveway, and Shannon rose and walked to the entryway to confront her husband. He entered the house with a smile and reeking of perfume. When he spotted Shannon, he came to a halt.

"So nice of you to arrive, Andrew. Over the last month, I wondered if you were working or having an affair. Still, considering your low libido and inability to perform, I doubted another woman would want you. It seems I was wrong. When were you going to find the courage to tell me?"

"You haven't been interested in me for over twelve months. Penny is interested in my job and supportive of my attempts to earn a promotion."

"Where did you meet this paragon of virtue?"

"There's no need to be snide. I met Penny at the conference."

Shannon lost her temper and shrieked, "No need to be snide? You've been cheating on me for months, and you are calling out my behaviour? You have wasted five years of my life while I scrimped and saved, and you spent a lot on incidentals because you earned more than I did. I wonder how soon Penny will get sick of never seeing you, of your limp dick and non-existent libido?"

Andrew's face turned a startling shade of red, and Shannon thought he might have a heart attack. Walking away from her cheating husband, she said. "In the morning, pack your bags and get out."

Shannon climbed into bed in the spare room, and the tears came. She sobbed until exhaustion gripped her, and she fell into a broken sleep.

When Shannon woke in the morning, she lay in bed, her eyes gritty and a headache dancing around her temples. With a sigh, she pulled herself from the bed and prepared for the morning. As soon as she stepped into the hallway, she knew something was different. The door to the main bedroom was open, and by the neat bed, it was evident that Andrew had not slept in their room. A quick check of the cupboards and drawers revealed only empty spaces. His books were missing, his vinyl records and CDs were gone, and his industry awards were missing as well. Shannon walked through the house, checking for Andrew's belongings; he had packed everything he could while she cried herself to sleep. The snake had slithered out during the night because he didn't dare to face her in the morning.

Shannon rang her work to say she needed a personal day and sat at the table with a notepad and pen to list the changes she needed to make now that Andrew had left. Her first call was to Andrew's mother to tell her that the marriage was over because her son had been cheating. After the conversation, Shannon felt sorry for the other woman; there was no greater failure than raising a self-involved, unfaithful man. She called her mother next, prepared for her to remind Shannon that she and her father had voiced their concern when the two young folks announced their engagement. Her mother surprised Shannon by suggesting that she had not given up on Andrew yet.

"Dear, sometimes men need to sort out their priorities. Andrew will put this little diversion behind him and return to you."

"Mother, Andrew can do whatever he wants, but it won't involve climbing into my bed, not that he was ever very active when he made it to bed. Believe me, I have no desire to be associated with the cheater. We had major issues that needed to be solved, but all he did was blame me, ignore the problem, and work longer hours. Our marriage is over, and no apologising or counselling will fix it."

Shannon needed a stiff drink after the frustrating call to her mother, but at ten in the morning, that would not help her get through the day. She had to make extensive changes, so sitting here and fuming over her mother's ridiculous advice wouldn't get her tasks done. The first call was to the couple's solicitor, and since he was a friend of Andrews', Shannon expected no help from him; the call was made to make a courtesy visit before she transferred her legal affairs to another business. Three hours later, Shannon shrugged as she left the office of the man who had been the couple's legal counsel for more than five years. She had expected nothing more from the man; he never seemed to take her concerns seriously and always referred to Andrew when they had to decide on options regarding their legal affairs. Shannon felt like she had broken out of a bad dream; it was time to get her life in order. Well, good riddance.

After phoning more prominent law firms in the district, which revealed that none had female partners, Shannon began looking at companies with smaller addresses on the website. Mandy Brewer was the principal at Brewer, Holt, and Pascoe. When she rang to make an appointment, she was surprised to discover that the business had three female solicitors, so she asked to speak to someone who could review her legal documents and lodge the divorce papers.

Shannon was staggered at the complexities of dissolving a marriage; there were insurance policies to alter, health insurance to change, and a new will to write. Shannon's final request was about changing her name by deed poll. By the end of the day, her new counsel, Mandy, had initiated the divorce proceedings and sent a letter to Andrew's lawyer, stating that her husband needed to continue depositing money into the joint account to cover bills related to the house.

By the end of the day, Shannon felt exhausted and wanted nothing more than to climb into bed. The need to tell Amelia and Beck what had transpired had her dial the familiar number to talk to her friend. After spending a few minutes updating their lives, Shannon had to confess to Amelia all that had happened. Stunned silence greeted Shannon, and for a moment, she thought she had lost the connection. Then, a stream of curse words filled the air as Amelia swore black and blue about the unfaithful bastard Andrew turned out to be. Shannon was thankful that Amelia didn't say what she must have been thinking; Andrew was always someone she didn't trust, and his poor treatment of Shannon and his cheating were not unexpected.

"What are you going to do now?"

Shannon relayed the details of her day, and Amelia murmured her approval. When Shannon told her about her mother's comments, Amelia was outraged.

"As if you want the bastard after five years of neglect and control and cheating as the final insult. You're well rid of him, although thinking of his new woman probably stings. Can you get time off? Come for a few days to get you away from the mess."

"I never took many holidays because Andrew said it would work well when we had children. What a laugh; I often wondered if he thought, because there had been one immaculate conception in history, we might get a second one. How was I ever going to have children with that man? I often speculated that he was gay and trying to cover himself with a wife and a middle-class lifestyle."

"The description of your sex life points to that. Do you want me to tell Beck?"

"Thanks. I've had enough of today. I'll ring you when I know what days I can take off."

Chapter Seven

Four months had passed since Andrew had walked out of Shannon's life, and after dealing with the legalities of the marriage, Shannon decided to take the holiday that Andrew had denied her for five years. The accumulated savings in her account paid for her trip to Western Australia, and as she wanted to make the most of her month in the West, she booked tours around the areas she wanted to see.

When she landed in Perth after the long flight, the car she had booked to deliver her to the motel sat outside, the driver holding a sign with her name. Despite her fatigue, she flashed the man a huge smile, and he blinked in surprise as he loaded her luggage into the boot. Her check-in at the motel was speedy, and she was alone in the room she had booked before she knew it. The urge to climb into bed assailed her, but she resisted the urge. First, she needed to eat, and then she had to contact the first tour company to confirm her booking.

Two weeks later, Shannon entered a room similar to every motel she had slept in during the tours of landmarks, tourist attractions and wineries. She reminded herself to review the tour itinerary next week, as she would cancel if it consisted of many wineries. It wasn't that Shannon disliked wine, but once you'd seen one winery, you'd seen them all. Given the nature of their business, the setup and marketing were similar, and she didn't want to waste her limited time. Shannon enjoyed her trip very much, and even after her four weeks were up, there would be areas she hadn't visited. She might have to consider another trip to the West.

After a shower and changing clothes, Shannon headed for the dining room. Diners packed the room, and Shannon knew the servers would frown upon a single customer taking up a table that could seat two or more. The only downside to travelling alone was that tours and dining areas seemed to cater for groups or couples, and if they made provision for a single diner, the table was near the toilets or outside the kitchen. Should she go for a walk and see if there were smaller eateries that would serve a lone customer? While considering her options, she wandered into the high-class tavern attached to the motel and asked the barman for a rum and cola. Lost in her thoughts, Shannon didn't see the man standing next to her until he spoke.

"Is this seat taken?"

Shannon shook her head and glanced sideways when he sat beside her. Holy moly, the guy next to her was good-looking, and he smelled like pine and something she couldn't distinguish.

"Are you waiting for someone?"

Shannon laughed. "No, I'm procrastinating."

"What is the dilemma? Maybe I can help."

Shannon shrugged. Did it matter if she confided in this stranger? She was unlikely to run across him after tonight. "I'm trying to decide if I should eat here and have the servers put me on a single table near the toilets or the kitchen, or go somewhere else. Even in this enlightened age, waitstaff don't like single diners."

"Ah, I see your point."

"Why are you propped at the bar? Are you waiting for someone?"

"I'm trying to hide from a cougar stalking me."

Shannon laughed. "I hate to tell you this, but a bar is not the best place to hide."

"If she sees me, can I pretend you're my girlfriend? The woman asked if I was married or engaged, but not if I had a girlfriend. Will you help if she arrives looking for me?"

"Are you married or engaged? Maybe we should exchange names so your ruse looks more authentic. Hello, I'm Shannon."

" I'm currently separated and have no other entanglements. My name is Jackson, but my friends call me Jax. Why don't we go for dinner, and I won't be a sitting duck?"

Shannon looked around the room and spied a woman making a beeline for Jaxon. "Your pursuer just discovered you. It's showtime."

Shannon pushed herself against Jackson as a woman called out, "Whoo hoo, Jackson. I finally found you."

With her fingers tangled in the hair at his nape, Shannon pulled him towards her, and their lips collided. The kiss, which Shannon meant to be brief but enough to deter the other woman, became fiery. As Jackson pressed for more than an open-mouthed kiss, Shannon groaned. The sound of the barman clearing his throat pulled them apart.

"Better take that elsewhere, mate."

Jackson laughed. "Do you want to grab that meal now?"

"Wow, that was some kiss! I think you fried my brain. Your pursuer has left, assuming she was the short, tubby blonde making a beeline for you."

After following the rules for the last five years, Shannon decided to join this attractive stranger and see where it went. Jackson tucked her hand in his crooked arm and led the way out of the bar, and Shannon wanted to press her fingers against her mouth to see if she could still taste him. She wondered whether Andrew's assessment of her was accurate and whether Shannon was a nymphomaniac, because Jackson's kiss sent a flurry of inappropriate thoughts through her mind. Could she sit opposite this man and pretend everything was normal while her hormones were on high alert? His low, rumbly voice pulled her out of her thoughts as he entered a restaurant she wouldn't have considered. The exterior of the building was uninspiring, and the interior was dim, with the tables along one wall.

"Are you sure this has edible food? "

"Certain. I discovered this place during my last visit to Perth. The décor leaves much to be desired, but the food is excellent. I hope you're not one of those women who order a salad and then push it around with your fork pretending to eat."

Shannon laughed. "Salad is a great side dish, but in my humble opinion, it is not a meal. There will be no food pushing; I'm famished."

Shannon and Jackson shared a series of dishes for the next hour and chatted about their lives and why they were in Perth. Jackson revealed that he was on business, and Shannon confided that she was rewarding herself after surviving the breakup of her marriage. A few questions from Jackson opened the floodgates. Shannon spilled the details of the end of her marriage and the tedious business of disentangling their lives when Andrew refused to talk to her, and all her questions had to get through his solicitor.

When she finished her rant, Shannon blushed and ducked her head.

"Sorry about that. Now and then, the unfairness of the situation hits me."

Jackson shook his head and said, "It never fails to amaze me how the person you promised to honour, forsaking all others until death do you part, manages to screw their partner over. My story is no prettier than yours; you wasted five years of your life, but my wife was screwing around only months after our wedding. When I challenged her, she said she needed an open marriage. She had never heard the word monogamy, and I didn't intend to share her with a series of other blokes. Why didn't I know this before the damn ceremony if that was the case?"

Shannon shook her head. "Aren't we sad sacks? Is it better to find out as you did at the beginning of the marriage rather than commit five years to a flawed relationship?"

Jackson signalled the waiter and handed him his black credit card when the man returned. As they strolled towards their motel, Jackson said. "Would you like to join me in my room for a nightcap?"

Shannon glanced at her handsome companion, and her mind returned to those inappropriate thoughts that had plagued her earlier. If she were to have a nightcap, she needed to know if the invitation was to spend the night or if it genuinely was a nightcap.

"Only if you make it worth my while."

Jackson grinned. "I promise to make it well worth your while."

Chapter Eight

As Jackson pushed his door open, nerves made Shannon rethink her decision. She watched as Jackson shed his suit jacket and tie, flicked off his shoes, and undid his belt. The slow striptease sent Shannon's hormones into overdrive, but she wondered if this decision was wise. She had never slept with anyone but Andrew, and it was lacklustre at best. Jackson watched as Shannon chewed her bottom lip, flushing as he removed his outer clothes.

"Have you changed your mind? We can have that drink if you prefer."

"I haven't changed my mind, but I'm worried I'll disappoint you. Andrew never managed to get very aroused, and sometimes he didn't finish. He said it was because I was too needy and accused me of being a nymphomaniac. It would mortify me if you couldn't perform because I lack sex appeal."

Jackson cupped her cheek with his hand and tilted her face towards himself.

"Shit. The guy did a number on you, and you gave him five years to undermine your self-belief. I assure you I will have no problem performing, and I will make tonight a night to remember."

Shannon let out a loud sigh.

"Okay, I trust you to make this memorable."

Jackson grinned as he removed her jacket and turned her to unzip her dress. When the silky material slid down to Shannon's waist, he licked his lips at the lacy bra that cupped her generous breasts. Jackson removed her embarrassment at being the focus of his attention when he placed his mouth on hers. The bartender ended their first kiss, but there was no one here to stop the fiery kiss that consumed her. Jackson's mouth moved to her neck, and she groaned as he nibbled and kissed her. When Shannon felt his hands cup her breasts, she realised that he had undone her bra and removed it while she swooned under the feeling of his lips.

"Let's take this to bed."

As Jackson lay her on the bed, she sighed. So far, this had been better than anything Andrew had managed during their marriage. Shannon watched as Jackson stripped off his shirt and removed his suit pants and socks. Her eyes ran over his body, taking in his defined arms, chest muscles, and tight stomach. God, he was gorgeous, and she intended to enjoy every minute in bed with him. Shannon shut thoughts of Andrew down as Jackson managed to pay attention to every inch of her body. She writhed on the bed, and after two orgasms, she was boneless and dreamy, but her desire ramped up when he slid into her.

"Open your eyes. I want you to know who is inside you."

Shannon opened her eyes, looking into his languid brown eyes, darkened with lust. Jackson moved slowly initially, and Shannon's body stretched to accommodate his length. Soon, though, she needed more and urged Jackson on with cries for more. With her legs wrapped around him and her nails digging into his buttocks, Shannon was entirely at his mercy, and she enjoyed every moment of their union. Jackson's body shuddered as he climaxed, and he lay over Shannon as he gained the strength to move. He rolled to the side and pulled her with him.

"Don't go anywhere; I need to dispose of the condom."

Shannon watched as Jackson got out of bed and walked, unconcerned about his naked state, to the bathroom. His tight butt, strong leg muscles, and well-developed frontals suggested he worked out regularly. Shannon approved whatever he did to make his body a work of art. Jackson slid into bed and pulled her towards him, arms wrapped tight around her.

"Can you stay the night?"

"You want more?"

"Sweetheart, I doubt one night will be enough. Have a nap because I will show you other positions apart from the missionary when I wake you."

Shannon sighed. "Thank you for proving I'm normal."

Jackson kissed her on the cheek, tucked her against his body, and they drifted off.

Shannon woke; her body vibrated with longing, and her pulse raced. The large hand that rested on her waist slipped down to her clit and ran along her wet folds. An involuntary moan escaped her lips, and she wriggled against the hard cock pressed against her. Jackson peppered her shoulders and back with kisses, and as she writhed against him, he moved her leg backward over his and slid into her with a soft groan. Shannon lay still for a heartbeat before moving against him, and Jax took over the pace with his fingers, driving her mad. When the orgasm thundered through her, Shannon lost all track of time and place, and it wasn't until Jax groaned that she could focus. She had never felt so content, and if this were only one night, as they had agreed, she would treasure the memories and store the feeling to remember in her old age. Although if she were being truthful, the memories of their time together would haunt her every day for years. Jax rolled out of bed, and Shannon vaguely remembered him returning to bed as she dozed.

The next time Shannon woke, the place in the bed next to her was empty, and before she could assume Jax had abandoned her, he walked into the room.

"Wake up, sleepy head. If you slip into your clothes and return to your room, I will give you thirty minutes to shower and change; I thought we could have breakfast together."

Shannon yawned, stretched, and saw Jackson's eyes darken before he shook his head and stepped back.

"You tempting wench! Get up now, or I'll tumble you into bed again, and I won't make my meeting."

Shannon grinned and scrambled out of bed.

"I never knew I had the power to distract a man, and it's a pretty heady feeling."

As she pulled on her clothes, she headed for the door.

"Oh, I'm on the third floor in room eighty-two."

Jackson nodded. "See you soon."

Chapter Nine

Shannon felt a sense of ease as they ate breakfast that she couldn't remember ever feeling before. Jax was easy to talk to, and although she guessed he must be financially well-off, he never talked down to her; his interest in what she had to say was genuine. They had agreed to a one-night stand, but the breakfast shattered that agreement; Shannon wondered whether she could encourage him to extend their intimacy until Friday, when she left. Before she could broach the subject, Jax raised the possibility of expanding their friendship.

"I know I said one night, but I like you, and I don't want to say goodbye when I can still see you in the hotel. Besides, I still have more positions to show you; we've just started."

Jax flashed her a brilliant smile, and Shannon laughed.

"How could I turn down such a generous offer? And I like you too. You may be a big wheel in business, but I feel comfortable talking to you. I would be pleased to join you in your suite later today."

"Good." Jackson rose from his seat.

"I have to go, or I will be late, and since I'm giving the keynote speech, it would be bad form. I'll see you this afternoon, and we can explore some more."

Shannon watched Jax walk away, and she pulled out her guidebook. She signalled the server for another cup of tea, and with the book opened in front of her, she began to circle the attractions she would like to see

Shannon spent the morning riding the trams and viewing significant sites and tourist attractions. She had lunch in the botanical gardens, shaded by century-old trees, and decided she liked this city's vibe. She could not have chosen a better reward for herself. Shannon grinned then, remembering the handsome man in whose bed she would spend the night. By early afternoon, her feet hurt, and Shannon could think of no better way to spend the remainder of the afternoon than lounging in the pool.

Hours later, when her skin had wrinkled, Shannon decided to dress for dinner and see if Jackson had finished his meeting. She heard a woman's gushing voice as she strode through the foyer towards the conference room. If she was not mistaken, it sounded like the cougar who was hunting Jackson. Shannon rounded the corner, and a group of people stood chatting, but the woman whom Jackson had been hiding from the first night they met had her hand firmly around his arm. He looked up as she walked towards the group and winked at him. When she reached him, she stretched to kiss him and then looked at the cougar.

"You are so kind to look after Jackson, but I'm sorry, I'm going to have to steal him as we've got an early reservation."

The woman released her grip on Jackson's arm and, with bad grace, stomped away.

"Will you excuse us, gentlemen?"

When the men wandered away, Jax said, "What is our early reservation?"

Shannon shrugged. "I couldn't think of any other way to rescue you. You did need rescuing, didn't you?"

"I most certainly did. I want to change out of my suit, and you'd better stay here because with you in the room, once I start taking off clothes, I might not stop. Do you want to visit the art gallery?"

"As long as I don't have to walk for miles. I swear I wore the leather off the sole of my sandals today. Okay, do you want to meet me in the bar?"

"Sure, but don't pick up any strange men."

Shannon grinned. "I've fulfilled my quota for this year."

With a drink cradled in her hand, Shannon sat at the bar while waiting for Jax. A deep, masculine voice near her ear caused Shannon to shiver.

"Is this seat taken?"

Shannon turned and said, "I'm waiting for my sexy companion, but you can sit here until he arrives."

When Jax growled, Shannon laughed.

"Ah, look! It's my sexy companion."

"You are a wicked woman. Are you ready to go? I've ordered a car, and after the gallery, you won't have to walk far for dinner because there are eateries around that area."

Sliding her hand around his arm, Shannon said, "Lead the way."

Their trip to the gallery fascinated Shannon because the exhibits were all created by local artists. The variety of displays was broad, covering everything from charcoal sketches to watercolours and oils. The gallery dedicated a separate room to sculptures, and the diversity of exhibits was evident in the paintings on display. Shannon, who knew little about painting techniques and sculpture methods, found the visit captivating. Jax was an intelligent companion, and the trip through the gallery wasn't a quick whirl but a leisurely walk filled with discussions about the artworks. Jax's willingness to chat and share information with her pleased Shannon because, in her married life, Andrew usually led their conversations and rarely shared details with her. It was nice to be with a man who appreciated her input in the chat.

After a few hours at the gallery, Jax directed them to a seafood restaurant. The nautical design of the place amused Shannon, but when it came to ordering food, the decisions were difficult because the menu held all her favourite seafood dishes. As she struggled to make a choice, Jax queried her.

"There's nothing that takes your fancy?"

"Everything takes my fancy! My favourites are on the menu, so I can't decide what to have." Shannon groaned.

Jax called the waitress over, and after a quick discussion, she left with their order.

"Most of the dishes on the menu are included on the taster platter so that you can have a little of everything."

Shannon chuckled. "Aren't you full of surprises? Who knew you could order a platter and have so many options?"

"Most places want their customers to leave satisfied and happy, so an unusual request doesn't generally upset them, especially if the end tab will be worthwhile."

An hour later, Shannon groaned.

"I'm so full you might have to roll me back to the motel."

"Give me a minute to fix the bill, and I'll order a car."

The drive to the motel was silent, and Shannon wondered what Jax was thinking. As the car parked at the front of the motel, Jax said, "Will you spend the night with me? I know we said one night, but I'm enjoying myself so much I don't want tonight to end."

Shannon grinned. "Will you make it worth my while?"

Jax kissed her neck and whispered, " I have more positions to show you."

When Shannon woke the following day, it was the same as the previous morning. While she showered in her room and changed her clothes, she hummed to herself. Who could have imagined when she headed out on her holiday that she would spend a lazy few days making love and enjoying the sights with a sexy guy? Whatever happened between them now, Shannon knew that she would not regret a moment of their time together. The time spent with Jax was a time capsule that was seamlessly integrated into her everyday life, yet it convinced her that somewhere in the world, a man like him was waiting for her to arrive in his life.

The next few days, they followed the same pattern as the first days. At night, after finishing his work, Jax went sightseeing and then to a restaurant to eat. They spent their night in bed and, in the morning, emerged like moths from a cocoon. Shannon knew their time together was running out because she had another tour booked for her last days in Western Australia. She regretted making the booking, but she had paid for the tour and had come to see a part of this big state, not the inside of a hotel room. Shannon ate breakfast with Jax, which had become their morning routine, and then headed to her room to collect her luggage. Jax walked with her to the entrance, waiting for the tour bus to arrive.

"I've got another four days here, and I'm going to miss your company."

"And I've got a tour where I won't have a moment's peace, but when I climb into bed each night, I'll feel lonely. I like you, Jackson Caruthers, and I'm glad we met. Thank you for being great company, and I don't just mean in bed."

As the bus pulled away, Shannon wondered if she had made the right choice, but spending more time with Jax would make the goodbye even harder. How fair was life that she would meet a man who made her heart beat faster and could make her laugh, and he lived on the other side of the country from her?

Chapter Ten

Shannon sighed. This second day of her tour was as unexciting as the previous day. When she booked, Shannon had inquired about winery visits, and the tour operator said that on the last day of the tour, the group would eat lunch at the Willows winery. There would be a tasting and a tour for those who wanted to see the winery's inner workings. Shannon had no interest in seeing yet another winery, so the tour itinerary suited her. However, sometime between her confirmation of the itinerary and the tour's start, the operator changed the tour to accommodate other people who wanted to visit most of the wineries in the area.

When the group stopped for the night, Shannon spoke to the guide about her disappointment at the changed itinerary.

"I can't understand that after confirming the route for the tour, you didn't check that all of your clients accepted the changes. When I booked, I specifically asked about visiting wineries and was told there was a single visit on the last day. So far, over the previous two days, all we've done is visit one winery after another and by the time we pulled in tonight, most of the passengers were drunk. What have you got organised for tomorrow?"

"Ah, we have a winery visit in the morning and touring before evening, where we have booked accommodation at the Grande winery for the night."

"Well, you can spend the next few hours organising transport back to Perth for me at your company's expense. You will be lucky if I don't give you a lousy review on your pathetic tour."

The disgruntled guide walked away, his phone to his ear. Shannon collected her meal and walked away from the revelry of the other travellers. She was not in the mood to tolerate drunken advances and suggestive remarks, and hoped the guide managed to get her transport to return to Perth.

It was nearly nine o'clock when Shannon checked in at the hotel where she had spent the great days with Jax. She wondered if he was still there, and as the receptionist refused to tell her, Shannon decided to shower and dress before knocking on the door to the room he had occupied when she left. Nerves jiggled in her stomach as Shannon walked along the hallway to Jax's previous room. How foolish would she feel if a stranger answered the door? Would Jax want to see her, even though he said he would miss her when she left?

After taking a deep breath, Shannon knocked on the door. A male voice yelled, and Shannon stood nervously waiting for the door to open. The door opened, and Jax stood there. Shannon realised that his expression wasn't one of welcome but shock, and he was wearing only trousers. His feet were bare, his shirt was missing, and his hair looked like someone's hands had tousled it.

"Ah, sorry. The tour was a bust, so I thought...."

Before she finished her explanation, a blond woman wearing only a dress shirt of Jax's strolled to the door. She placed her hand possessively on Jax's arm and said

"Sorry, honey. I don't do threesomes."

Shannon flushed bright red and turned to flee along the hallway. She pushed the button on the escalator as the door to Jax's room closed. Shannon threw herself on her bed. She was a fool, thinking Jax would be happy to see her. Didn't Shannon pick him up at the bar? Of course, once she left, he would replace her with another eager woman. When the tears stopped, she decided to change motels so that, however long she remained here, she wouldn't see him with another woman.

The plane hit the tarmac with a squeal of tyres, and Shannon breathed a sigh of relief. She had enjoyed her first holiday in over five years and had come to terms with what she felt was Jax's desertion. Shannon knew that initially, their hook-up was supposed to be one night, and even though they had seen each other for five days, there was never any intention to continue their association. Shannon knew she would fondly remember her time with Jax and move forward with her life, knowing that she had normal sexual responses and Andrew was wrong, calling her a nymphomaniac.

Once her bags came around on the carousel, Shannon dodged the foot traffic until she reached the pickup area. A man with her name on a board held high was a welcome sight, and with her luggage stowed in the boot, they weaved through the traffic towards her house. After selling the home she and Andrew owned, Shannon had enough money to buy a modest brick veneer adjacent to the university grounds. Her property was suitable for sharing, and to help with costs, she rented two of her rooms to students. The two bathrooms were welcome because having three women in one house attempting to get ready for classes or social events would have been problematic. Shannon liked the girls who shared her home, although she felt she had returned to her student days when she shared a house with Amelia and Bree. The thought of her friends reminded her that soon she would have to ring them and fill them in on her holiday, but first she needed to organise herself to return to work tomorrow.

Shannon welcomed her return to work because she had too much spare time, which made her remember the time she spent with Jax. Try as she might, she missed him, and even though her friends attempted to get her to socialise, she couldn't get up the enthusiasm to participate. Her family also wanted to see her, and Shannon finally accepted an invitation to eat at her parents' house. It had been months since she had eaten with her parents because, even though Andrew had moved out, her mother insisted that he might change his mind and that she should be receptive to an apology. If the mad woman started tonight with her advice, Shannon vowed to leave and not return anytime soon.

When she arrived, it became clear this was a family meal. Her brother had parked in the driveway, and she knew she would have to run the gauntlet of questions about her marriage breakup and the holiday. Shannon greeted her brother and his wife, as well as her sister, who sat glued to the television and went in search of her mother. She helped dish food and carried platters into the dining room, and then her mum called the others to the table. The conversation remained general and light chit-chat until they cleared the desert and retired to the lounge room with their cups of tea and coffee. Her mother was the first to ask about Andrew. Shannon huffed and said,

"Mum, do I have to speak slowly so you understand what I say?"

"There's no need to be sarcastic, Shannon."

"It appears that there is a reason. Andrew spent five years refusing to go on holidays, refusing to let me spend money and making all the decisions regarding our future. Because he earned more money than I did, he spent money on football, cricket, and drinking with his mates, while I couldn't afford the cost of a haircut or a new dress without an inquisition. After suffering criticism and slurs for five years, he went off and slept with some other woman. He left me the night of our fifth anniversary, and even if he came crawling on hands and knees, I have no intention of ever forgiving him."

Before her mother could respond, Tammy, her brother's wife, said, " I agree. I would boot him out if Chris did that to me, and forgiveness would never be a consideration. Mrs Westcott, marriage was sacred in your time, but nowadays, women can move on and make a new life for themselves. The marriage breakdown was not Shannon's fault, and you shouldn't expect her to compromise her integrity for Andrew."

Chris stepped into the awkward silence that followed Tammy's support of Shannon, asking for details on Western Australia. Shannon told everyone what she had done and the things she had seen, avoiding all mention of Jax. She would talk to her friends about the man she met, but did not intend to share their antics with her family.

Chapter Eleven

Shannon's life was a combination of work, activities and meals with family and friends. Still, as she went through her days, memories of Jax popped into her mind with annoying regularity, and she would miss the conversations around her. On a night out with her workmates, Ben, the surgical resident, called her out on her distraction.

"Are you having man problems, or is your lack of focus due to something else? Since you returned from your holiday, you seem distracted; did something happen in the West?"

Ben asked the question quietly so that the entire table wasn't privy to it, and Shannon guessed that confiding in someone at work wouldn't be a bad thing. While she debated how to start the conversation, Ben said, " Come over to the bar with me, and I'll get us a drink. It might be easier to talk without the rabble surrounding us."

With a drink in front of them, Shannon began her tale. She told Ben about meeting Jax, having fun together, sightseeing, dining, and going to bed.

"Do I guess that the man might be Mr Right, but in the wrong place?"

"Yeah. I knew that my life was here and his life was in Western Australia, but I didn't think our time together would haunt me as it does. There are always what-if questions, and you can drive yourself mad trying to sort through the possibilities, but still, he interrupts my life."

"Is there a possibility of reuniting?"

Shannon grimaced. "When my last tour was a bust, I returned to the hotel hoping to reconnect with him, and he was with another woman."

"Okay, that's a no for now, but don't rule him out forever if you think he is Mr Right. My husband, Alex, wasn't ready to come out when we met. When I wanted to take the relationship further, he still wasn't prepared. We broke up for six months, and I tried to move on, but it's hard to do once you meet the right person. Thankfully, he missed me as much as I did and came out to his family and workmates. It wasn't all plain sailing because while his mum was disappointed but accepting, his father raged about his son being gay. When the dust settled, we married and are blissfully happy. If you think your Jax is Mr Right, don't push him away because he was with another woman. There may be reasons; if he wants to explain, listen with an open heart. If Alex refused to listen when I tried to explain my hook-ups while we were apart, I wouldn't have the happy marriage I have now."

Ben's advice stayed with Shannon as she moved through the week. While juggling her feelings about Jax and her mother's persistent attempts to reconcile Andrew and her, Shannon tried to avoid her family. Shannon relented when her mother begged her to come for a family dinner for Mother's Day. As she pulled up, the presence of a strange car raised her suspicions, but, giving her mother the benefit of the doubt, she entered the house by the front door. With a shake of her head, Shannon knew that berating her mother for leaving the door unlocked would get no response. Her mother's idea of security was snibbing the wire door, so Shannon let the matter slide. Walking through the house, Shannon arrived at the kitchen, where platters and food trays were spread out on the bench.

"Ah, good, you're here, Shannon. We can take the food into the dining room. Can you call the men to the table, Tammy?"

Once everyone was seated, Shannon glanced at the space set up for a guest, but it was vacant. The slam of the screen door announced the arrival of another person, and when Andrew entered the room, Shannon stiffened. How could her mother do this to her? As Andrew approached her, she glared at her former husband, who gave her a small smile.

"Don't be angry, Shannon. It's Mother's Day, and where else would I be but here with family?"

He leant towards her, and she suspected he was about to kiss her in greeting, but she pushed her chair away from the table.

"You have your parents; why aren't you with them?"

"I always have lunch here and dinner with my folks."

Shannon sneered. "I'm surprised you have time to eat here when you need to eat with Penny's parents."

Andrew's face flushed, and he said, "Penny and I are not together. I made a mistake with Penny and hoped you and I might try to reconnect."

Kathy Westcott smiled. "Shannon, I said that Andrew would come to his senses. You need to put this behind you and forgive him."

"Mother, you don't know what I suffered during our marriage, and while I don't want to air our dirty laundry in public, nothing less will convince you. We had to save almost every penny we made, and if I was foolish enough to buy a shirt or go to the hairdresser, Andrew blamed me for spending unnecessarily. When he and his mates got together every Saturday for football or cricket, her could spend whatever he wanted because he earned more than I did. He spent most of his life working and called me a nymphomaniac for wanting sex more than once a week. Our sex life was so dismal that Andrew scheduled it every Sunday, after dinner, in bed in the missionary position. My life was lonely and miserable, and I will never put myself under his control again. If you wish to have Andrew as your son, you lose me as your daughter."

Leaving her stunned family in her wake, Shannon heard her brother's incredulous question.

"Once a week? In the missionary position? Are you kidding me? It's a wonder Shannon wasn't cheating on you."

When the door banged behind her, it cut off Andrew's explanation, but it didn't matter what he said as an excuse because she no longer cared. Before she unlocked her car door, she heard her brother call her name. She turned to see what he wanted, only to realise Tammy was with him.

"You guys don't have to leave just because I am."

Tammy snorted. "We wouldn't have come, and I'd have warned you if we knew your mother invited that weasel."

Chris shook his head. "I can't get over the revelation that he scheduled sex once a week. What the hell?"

Shannon grimaced. "He made me feel unattractive and needy. His lack of interest in bed made me wonder if he was gay, but then he started his affair with that chick Penny and I felt like our poor sex life was down to me."

Tammy smiled. "The man's a fool; your mother isn't much smarter. You need to get dolled up, go to a bar, pick up some random man, and have hot and heavy sex."

Chris looked uncomfortable, and Shannon had a moment's indecision before she said,

" I did, and I did when I was in Perth. My hook-up laid to rest my concern that I was the problem, not Andrew."

Tammy squealed her approval, and Chris grimaced.

"I don't want to hear about your sex life; it makes me feel squeamish, but I have to say good for you."

Shannon grinned. "Let me know when you have time to get together, and we'll meet at the pub."

Tammy and Shannon swapped numbers, and they promised to catch up soon.

Chapter Twelve

Shannon slumped in her chair; today had been hectic, and tomorrow didn't look any more promising. When someone rang in sick, it meant those on the wards had to cover their patients, and with only so many hours in the day, luxuries like lunchtime and morning tea became redundant. How was it possible for one person to have three individual sick days in a week? The ringing phone jolted Shannon awake, and she shook her head. Once she answered, whoever had disturbed her sleep, she would shower and fall into bed.

"Hello, this is Shannon."

"Hi, Shannon. It's Jackson Caruthers speaking."

Shannon's breath caught in her throat, and her heart stuttered. What was she supposed to say?

"Shann, I know this call is out of the blue, but I need to see you. I am in Melbourne from Thursday to Monday morning and hope we can catch up."

"This call is a surprise. Why don't you tell me whatever you have to say over the phone?"

"I could, but I need to see you. Please meet me; this isn't a booty call, although I'd be a liar if I said I didn't want you. I miss you and want to see and talk to you."

Shannon deliberated for a moment.

"My brother and sister-in-law will be at the Pioneer Hotel on Coburg Street on Friday night. We'll be there at about six o'clock, so why don't you meet me there?"

"I can do that. See you then."

When Shannon ended the call, she was both surprised and excited. Her heart rejoiced to see Jax again, but her head told her she was asking for trouble. However, try as she might, Shannon had no willpower when it came to Jackson Caruthers. How could seeing the man who haunted her dreams and interrupted her day improve the situation?

A week later, when Shannon entered the Pioneer, the hostess asked if she had booked a table. With her affirmative answer, the hostess led her through the large dining area to the back section of the room. Chris and Tammy sat at the table, and after greeting her brother and sister-in-law, Tammy took a seat. Her gaze slid over the table, and her brow raised at the empty place already laid with cutlery and bread plates.

"Who else did you invite?"

Tammy shrugged. "We thought you must have invited someone else. I'm not sure why we must share a table with other customers, but that must be what is happening."

"Oh, no, " Chris groaned.

A quick look over her shoulder revealed the reason for Chris's dismay. Her mother, father and sister walked through the door and headed their way.

"This was a lovely idea. I enjoy a meal much more if I don't have to cook it."

"Mum, how did you know we were eating here?"

"Oh, that nice girl Diedre, who takes the bookings, rang and asked if we were joining you because she needed to organise the tables."

Shannon scowled. "Well, hell. Next time, we will go somewhere else because we have organised a meal together, and the topic of Andrew won't arise. And we figured the only way to do that was by not inviting you."

When the server arrived with the menu, she noticed the tension at the table, but having worked there for some time, she knew better than to ask if everything was alright. Everyone ordered drinks and a meal, and when the food arrived, the table's occupants made small talk and chatted about things that wouldn't cause conflict. Shannon had begun to relax when Andrew entered the room, and after scanning the tables, he made a beeline for them. Shannon had sat facing the door so she could see when Jax arrived, but the clear view of her former husband walking towards their table made her fume. Turning to look at her mother, she said, "Damn you, Mum. Tammy, Chris, and I wanted to have a meal together, and not only have you pushed your way in, but you've also invited Andrew."

Before she could storm out, Shannon's phone rang.

"Hi, Shann, I'm out the front."

"Meet me just inside the door. We aren't staying; I'll explain later."

Shannon pushed her chair away from the table and stood.

"Tammy and Chris, I will catch up with you, and we'll have a meal somewhere the staff aren't nosy. Right now, I have somewhere else to go."

As she strode to the door, Jax entered the room. The sight of him almost immobilised her, but the interested looks from the female customers forced her forward. Standing near him, she said, "God help me; you're as gorgeous as I remember."

Jax stepped closer and ran his knuckles along her cheek. His touch made Shannon close her eyes against the sensation, and he said, "I missed you, Shann."

He opened his arms, and she stepped into his embrace, her head resting against his heart and her arms locked around him. For Shannon, it felt like coming home.

"What the hell is happening here? Who is this man? Unhand my wife, buster."

Jax surveyed Andrew with a neutral expression, then turned to Shannon.

"Shann, does this man have any say about who you associate with?"

"No, he doesn't. Andrew, fuck off. You didn't want me before, and I don't want you now."

Jax linked his fingers with Shannon's, and they walked to the exit. Shannon didn't look back, but she could imagine Andrew standing with the same astonished look as when she first told him to go. As Jax opened the door of the waiting car, Shannon said, "Don't think you get a free pass because Andrew is an ass."

"That's fine because I have questions for you."

The car dropped them off at an Italian restaurant, and after Jax helped her out, he escorted her to the door. The hostess seated them immediately, and their table sat in a private alcove that Shannon guessed Jax had requested. They placed a drink order and, before they could begin their conversation, the server arrived with menus and said she would return in a few minutes. Not willing to discuss private business in front of an audience, they ordered their meal and waited for the server to deliver it.

Shannon felt like pinching herself to see if she was awake. Not in her wildest dreams did she imagine seeing Jax again, and certainly not in Melbourne. Shannon kept glancing at her handsome dinner companion as they ate, wondering when he would explain his visit. Halfway through their meal, Jax said, "Can I ask questions and give explanations later?"

Shannon nodded. "Sure."

"Why were you at the pub with your ex?"

"My mother keeps pushing me to reconcile with Andrew, who is no longer with the chick he had an affair with. At the last family dinner, Mum invited Andrew, so when I walked out, my brother and his wife left as well. We decided to catch up without my parents and Andrew being present, and booked a table. The nosey chick who takes the bookings rang Mum to discover if she, Dad, and Camille were coming, and that's how they knew where we were. And, of course, Mum invited Andrew. I'm unsure how to make her understand that our marriage was on the rocks even without the affair. I spelled out the problems in our marriage, but she still believes I should forgive him."

" Okay, from your comments, it didn't look like you want to reconcile, but I don't want to get in the middle of a reunion."

"There will be no reunion, now or in the future. I will never reunite with the controlling, undersexed twit that is Andrew. I wish her luck if he finds another woman gullible enough to take him."

"Do you want dessert?"

"No."

Jax signalled the server that he wanted the cheque, and when he paid, he escorted Shannon to the car waiting outside.

"Where are we going?"

"We can have coffee at the motel, and I can explain why I'm here and what you think happened with that other woman. You are safe; I won't make a move on you unless you ask, but I want privacy to argue my case."

Chapter Thirteen

The car slowed as the Regency Hotel came into sight. Neither occupant spoke as they climbed from the vehicle and entered the foyer. The walk along the quiet corridors was silent as Shannon and Jackson considered their next moves. Jax slid the keycard into the door and held it open for Shannon to enter. He shrugged off his suit jacket, pulled off his tie and shoes and rolled his sleeves. Memories of the last time Jax did this flashed through Shannon's mind, and she flushed. Shannon was finding it hard to keep her hands off Jax, but she wanted to hear what he had to say before she made any decisions about sleeping with him again.

Once Jax had made the drinks, he patted the couch so Shannon could sit beside him. After a few sips from his cup, Jax turned to Shannon.

"When you left Perth for the tour, I missed you. I missed you every time I walked the hallway, went to the bar or ate in the dining room. A few times, I heard a laugh or saw a brunette walk past, and I stopped what I was doing to check it wasn't you. I couldn't get you out of my brain, so I decided to sleep with another woman and purge you that way. I chose a woman who looked nothing like you. You saw the chick; she was blond, tall, and skinny. We had intended to have a one-night stand, but it didn't work out. I wasn't interested at first, and when you arrived, I had just told her I was sorry, but it wasn't working for me, and she should leave. She pulled that stunt with my shirt, and I knew what you thought. After finally getting rid of her, I tried to contact you, but you weren't answering your phone, and the receptionist wouldn't tell me which room you were in. The following day, I went to the room you had occupied the first time, but a woman answered the door, and eventually, reception told me that you had checked out earlier."

Jax took a sip from his cup, and Shannon tilted her head.

"So why are you here?"

Jax sighed. "After my failed hook-up, I decided that lots of work would remove the memory of you, but even if I worked twelve hours a day and fell into bed exhausted, you arrived in my dreams."

He gave a rueful chuckle. "I'm getting RSI in my hand from jerking off every morning in the shower. Trying to pretend you don't exist doesn't work, so I wanted to present a proposal if you feel like I do."

"Aren't we a hopeless pair? My work colleague, Ben, asked what the problem was as I zoned out of half the conversations around me. Ben told me about his breakup and how he and his partner reunited. He assumed something had happened in Western Australia, but didn't know what, and asked if I wanted to confide in him. I would have agonised over answering the phone when I saw the call was from you if Ben hadn't made me promise to allow you to explain."

"Remind me if I ever meet Ben to thank him."

"So, where do we go from here?"

Jax raised his arm. "Shan, come here."

Shannon slid under his arm and tucked herself into his side.

"I can't forget you, and after two months without you, my family and business associates asked if I was going through a change of life. The first time we met, you mentioned that your trip was your first holiday in five years. Have you got enough left to take some long weekends?"

"Ah, sure, but I couldn't fly to Western Australia and back even in a long weekend. I'd spend more time in the plane than with you."

"You're right, so I suggest we meet in Adelaide. It's not exactly halfway, but it's closer for us both, and you and I would have less flying to do and, on a long weekend, more time together. It probably isn't a long-term solution, but it is my best suggestion."

"I want to do that, and I'm sure I can wrangle some time off, but I couldn't afford too many trips."

"I'll pay your airfares. If you text or email me when you have time off, I'll have my assistant book the tickets and arrange for a car to pick you up at the airport. If you're okay with that, I'll get her to book a motel away from the main thoroughfare."

"Can we do this?"

"A long-distance relationship is tricky, but I'm unwilling to let you get away a second time."

Shannon climbed onto Jax's lap, straddling his knees. He cupped her face and said, "Shan, I missed you so much, and I want to explore how far this attraction can go.

"You, Jackson Caruthers, are the stranger I can't forget. Let's do this."

The conversation ended there because Jax kissed her, and the fire he ignited never seemed to dim. Shannon ground against him, eliciting groans from them both. Jax stood, and Shannon wrapped her legs around him as he walked them to the bedroom. After two months apart, he struggled to control himself, but when Shannon urged him to forget the preliminaries and enter without delay, he complied. They knew they would spend most of the weekend in bed, so savouring their interaction could come later, but their need was urgent.

The weekend went too quickly for Shannon. This visit was Jax's first time in Melbourne, so Shannon gave him a tourist's view of the city on Saturday and Sunday. Neither was looking forward to him leaving, but they had obligations in their respective cities they couldn't ignore. When Shannon woke on Monday morning, the sight of Jax in casual clothes, ready for his flight, made her want to weep. He wheeled his suitcase to the door and laid his suit bag on the case as he walked back to sit on the edge of the bed. Gently pushing the hair from Shannon's face, he said,

"Promise me you won't get cold feet and change your mind about meeting me in Adelaide."

Shannon cupped his face with her hands and kissed him.

"There is no way I will change my mind. I will see you in a month."

Jax nodded and walked towards the door. He grinned as he said, "You'd better get out of bed, or you will be late for work."

Shannon nodded, and then the door closed behind him. How would she survive for another month before she saw Jax again? Once Shannon showered and changed, she walked through the foyer towards the entrance. Her weekend interlude was over, and she had to re-enter the real world.

"Excuse me, are you Shannon Westcott?"

The query was unexpected, and Shannon swung around to face the receptionist.

"Yes, yes, I am."

"Mr Carruthers ordered a car for you. The driver is waiting for you in the pickup area."

Shannon smiled; of course, he had ordered a car for her. She thanked the receptionist and left the building with a warm feeling. This man was so sexy, sweet and thoughtful that Shannon knew her heart was at stake, and for the first time, she didn't care. She would go forward with this connection and see where it led because her sensible choice of a man sentenced her to five years of frustration and indifference, and ended in betrayal. This time, she intended to follow her heart and pursue the deep attraction between her and Jax.

Chapter Fourteen

When Jax's plane touched down, he felt a surge of satisfaction. He had not only tracked Shannon down but had explained the circumstances of their last meeting and received her understanding. After his failed marriage, Jax didn't want to move too quickly, but he couldn't erase Shannon from his mind, and the trip to Melbourne was to ask her forgiveness and see if he had built up their attraction in his mind. As soon as Shannon walked towards him in the pub, he knew that the interest was genuine, and he wanted to see if their attraction was enough to build a relationship. His marriage to Marissa was more of a business deal than a love match, but Jax liked her, and they were good in bed, but she never looked at him like Shannon did. Marissa hid her feelings, and often, Jax felt that his wife was playing a part; after the wedding, her true character was revealed. Marissa cared nothing for him, and while she wanted the title of Mrs Carruthers, she didn't like everything else that went with it.

Once he arrived at work, Jax pushed thoughts of his estranged wife aside and focused on the numerous emails and phone messages that had accumulated during his weekend with Shannon. Jax checked his calendar for next month to check his obligations, noting the weekends Shannon might choose. He should discuss with Grace, his assistant, making arrangements when Shannon called or emailed. Grace had been with Jax since starting the business, and at her advanced age, she had comforted Jax after witnessing the destruction of Jax's marriage. Pushing the button on his intercom, he said, "Grace, can you come in? Bring a pad and pencil." The request was unusual, as they generated most of their work on computers; so, when his assistant walked in, she gave him a curious look.

"What can I do for you, Jax?"

Jax ran his hand through his hair, and a moment passed before he spoke.

"You know, I went to Melbourne for that buyer's conference? I attended because I wanted to see a woman I met the last time I was in Perth. My track record with women is poor, as evidenced by my failed marriage, but something about this woman makes her unforgettable. We spent five days together in Perth while she was on holiday, and I wanted to see if I had built her up in my mind and if she was not as remarkable as I remembered."

"So, what happened?"

Jax groaned. "She is more wonderful than I remembered. Her name is Shannon Westcott, and she has separated from her husband of five years. I met the man; he is a fool. She is pretty, not stunning like Marissa, and open and honest. She would make a lousy poker player because you can read her face like a book. We enjoy each other's company; when she was in Perth, I played tour guide, and last weekend in Melbourne, she did the same. I made a proposal she agreed to, so this is where you come in."

"So, I send lots of flowers and jewellery?"

"The flowers might be a nice touch, but forget the jewellery; she's not likely to be swayed by expensive gifts. We've decided to have a long-distance relationship. Once a month, we will both fly to Adelaide and spend a long weekend. Shannon will email or text to let me know when she can get the time off, and I'll need you to book her business class on the earliest flight out and the latest flight back. We will need a room at a motel and a car at our disposal, and that time in Adelaide needs to be clear of interruptions."

"How long do you envisage this relationship to continue? Does she know you're wealthy?"

"Yes, she knows I'm well-heeled; after all, we met at one of the best hotels in Perth. Shannon was staying there as part of a package deal, but we didn't go to expensive restaurants or spend a fortune on champagne or other things. I'm certain she isn't interested in my money. We will continue our rendezvous until one of us tires of the other or until it gets serious, and then we will have to talk about where we want to live."

"I can make those arrangements for your friend, but might I say I am gobsmacked? You have model-type women falling over themselves to accompany you to fundraisers and social events, and suddenly, you are making plans with a new woman."

"Ah, that is something else I need help with. I need non-threatening women to take to social events because Shannon and I are exclusive. I will take Dana whenever she is in town, and there's a function, but for the times my sister is in Albany, I will need women who aren't flashy and don't want to be in the spotlight by wearing hardly any clothes."

"Um, the non-threatening women might be the biggest challenge, but I'll see what I can do. What makes this woman stand out? After Marissa, I thought you'd sworn off relationships."

"Marissa certainly made me reconsider committing to another woman, but Shannon is different. All the models and women in society are aware of my net worth, which, in their eyes, makes me a suitable candidate. Shannon has no idea who I am or how much I'm worth; she likes me for who I am. She is open and friendly, and we have plenty to discuss and enjoy together. She makes me laugh, and I can't be in her presence without touching her."

"Well, if this woman is the one to make you cut back on work and live a little, I'm all for your long-distance relationship. I'll do whatever

I can to make the visits as stress-free as possible, and I look forward to hearing from her."

Shannon counted down the days until she flew to Adelaide. After spending three days in Melbourne with Jax, Shannon hoped their connection would remain strong, as she had quickly become hooked on the guy. The thought of seeing Jax again made her both excited and nervous. After putting her life back together when Andrew walked out, Shannon enjoyed the life she had built. Her job gave her great satisfaction, and Shannon liked most of her fellow employees. She frequently wished that Amelia and Beck lived closer, but she decided to drive the four hours once a month and stay overnight with them. Shannon had filled her weeknights with activities she had joined to alleviate loneliness in her marriage, and she had made friends with other women who also participated. Still, nothing beats spending time with her best friends.

Once a week, Shannon met her brother, Chris, and his wife, Tammy, at an out-of-the-way restaurant. She enjoyed not sharing the table with Andrew and not having to listen to her mother tell her about Andrew's redeeming qualities, which made for a more relaxed evening. A week before she was due to fly to Adelaide, Chris asked her about Jackson.

"Sis, what do you know about this Jackson guy? I worry that you will arrive in Adelaide and find he isn't who you think he is. "

"Big bro, I met this guy in Perth because he was at a conference in the same hotel where I was staying. We spent five days together, and then spent time together when he came to Melbourne. I think neither of us could believe the instant attraction, and so his trip was, in part, an apology for something that happened after I went on the last tour, and also to check if the appeal was as strong as we remembered. Please don't worry; I know plenty about Jax because we spend almost as much time talking as we do in bed."

Tammy laughed at Shannon's comment, but Chris growled.

"Big brothers do not need that kind of information about their little sister."

Shannon joined Tammy as the women laughed, reminding Shannon how much she liked Chris's wife.

After her conversation with Tammy, Shannon was in a better mood than when she had left her parents' house. However, her mother's constant comments about reuniting with Andrew confused and angered her. Why couldn't her Mother understand that she had spent five years working toward Andrew's dream and losing herself in the process? Shannon's decision to end the marriage the night of their wedding anniversary was something she had considered numerous times during their time together; his infidelity gave her the push she needed to end their toxic relationship.

Chapter Fifteen

As Shannon walked through the airport to the baggage collection area, she looked for someone with a sign with her name. It seemed to take an eternity for her suitcase to appear, and as she swung around to find her ride, her gaze fell on the handsome man walking towards her. She pulled her case behind her as she hurried towards Jax, and he hugged her when she was close enough.

"God, woman, you are a sight for sore eyes. Let's get out of here."

"I thought someone random would pick me up. When did your plane land?"

"We landed an hour ago, so I grabbed a quick drink while I waited."

Shannon reached to collect her case, and Jax grabbed the handle before she could get it. With their hands entwined, the couple moved towards the exit, and as they prepared to leave, a female voice called out, "You who, Jackson?"

With a sigh, Jax turned, keeping Shannon tucked firmly against himself. They stood together as a woman approached, her lips pouted and a slight frown on her face.

"Jackson, darling, you didn't call me after we spent the night together like you said you would. I see you are busy now, but I hope you can call me when you finish with your little friend."

Jax felt Shannon stiffen against him, but before he could speak, she said, "Honey, you look smart enough to work out that if a guy says he will ring you and doesn't, it means he has no wish to reconnect. You can wait until Jackson finishes with me if you like, but you might be an old hag by then because we won't finish any time soon."

The woman's eyes widened, and then she glared at Shannon as she walked away. Shannon heard a chuckle and looked up at Jax. His face crumpled when their eyes met, and his full-bellied laugh made her shake her head.

"Bravo, sweetheart. I don't need security when you are around."

Shannon wondered if she should question Jax about the woman as they walked to the car. Didn't they agree on being exclusive? Jax tossed her suitcase in the boot and opened the door for her.

"Shann, I know what you're thinking, but we agreed on being exclusive, and I will honour that agreement. I have no idea who that chick was because I don't visit Adelaide often, and the last time I was here, I was in meetings all day. You know, I wasn't exactly a saint after my marriage imploded, but I haven't been with a woman since well before I met you. Endless hookups with women whose names I never bothered to find out had lost their appeal months before I met you. I agreed to a one-night stand with you because I genuinely liked and found you interesting. Are women coming onto me going to be a problem?"

"I guess I feel a little unworthy of a hot, sexy guy like you, and after Andrew cheated, I'm not as trusting as I was. Women hitting on you will only be a problem if you respond."

Jax grinned. "You think I'm hot and sexy?"

Shannon snorted. "Don't you have any mirrors in your place? You're smokin' hot, which is why women fluff their hair and push out their boobs as you walk past."

"So when we arrive at the motel, will you fluff your hair and push out your boobs?"

"No, I'm going to start by unbuttoning your shirt and undoing your belt, and I'll go on from there."

Jax groaned. "I like your thinking."

Shannon barely made it through the suit's door when Jackson pushed her against the wall and devoured her mouth with his. His desperation urged Shannon to pull at his clothes and wrap her legs around his waist. As he opened her shirt to reveal her breasts, Shannon ground her hips against him. Through the thickness of their clothes, she could feel Jackson's erection pressing against her, and she groaned in frustration.

"Please, Jax, I need you."

Jackson continued to kiss Shannon, but while she writhed against him, he slid his hand into the top of her pants. He slid his fingers through her wet folds and circled her clit.

"Do you want to come?"

"Yes, yes, yes."

Jax's fingers, slick with her juices, circled her clit and then rubbed lightly.

"Harder, Jax, harder."

Within minutes, Shannon stiffened against him and then moaned loudly. Jackson watched Shannon's face with satisfaction; her mussed hair and flushed face were the best things he had seen in a month, and he intended to repeat this sight many times over the next four days. As Jax slid her to the ground, Shannon grabbed his belt.

"Your turn."

Jax shook his head.

"I want us in bed, naked. We aren't going anywhere until I've feasted on you, and when you are satiated, I will fuck you until you scream my name."

As Jackson put his threat into practice, the only thought that flittered through Shannon's mind was that she had fallen hopelessly in love with Jackson. The trick would be to let him make her mindless in bed without blurting out her feelings. Shannon dozed in Jax's arms until hunger roused her from her pleasant cocoon. Jax pushed her hair away from her face and kissed her gently.

"Are you hungry?"

"Mmm."

Jackson laughed. "Was that an affirmative mmm, or a negative?"

"Mr Caruthers, I will say that I am starving to clarify the issue. What kind of man works his girlfriend so hard without feeding her?"

"Are you my girlfriend?"

Shannon blushed. "Er, I sort of thought I was?"

"I'm teasing. I would be honoured to have you as my girlfriend. Let's hit the shower, and then we'll find somewhere to eat."

The shower took quite some time because Jax got sidetracked, and another round of lovemaking ensued before they left their room.

Shannon's four days with Jax flew by. During the day, they played tourists, then dined at one of the numerous restaurants and eateries, and retired to their room.

On their last day together, they planned their next getaway and booked a hotel room before leaving. Jax's plane left before Shannon's, and she prayed she could wave him goodbye without bursting into tears. Their days together were like a dream; sometimes Shannon needed to pinch herself to make sure she was awake. While Jax checked his luggage, the girl at the counter flirted blatantly, and Shannon gritted her teeth as she watched the interaction. When the woman reached out her hand to touch Jake, his instinctive move away cheered her. The woman raised her eyebrows, and Jax moved closer and whispered in her ear. When the woman blushed, Shannon wanted to gnash her jaws together, but as Jax moved towards her with a grin, Shannon wondered what he had told the woman.

"Do you want to share the amusing secret you whispered to the check-in chick?"

"Jealous, sweetheart?"

"Yes, and if you want to share, this conversation could end badly for you and her."

Jax wrapped his arm around Shannon's waist and kissed her forehead.

"I told her I was gay. Nothing kills the interest if a woman thinks the man she is making eyes at is in the other team."

Shannon laughed. "You are horrible, but I'm pleased you killed her interest. Let's walk you down to the waiting area, and when you go through security, I'll check in my bags."

They walked silently towards the other end of the terminal, and Jax pulled Shannon towards himself when an influx of travellers threatened to separate them. When the tannoy in the airport announced that passengers flying to Perth were boarding, Jax turned Shannon to face him.

"Saying goodbye doesn't get any easier. I miss you every second we are apart. I'll talk to you soon, okay?"

Shannon had promised herself she wouldn't cry when Jax left, but as the tears welled, it was a near thing.

"Jackson Carruthers, how I was lucky enough to meet you that night at the bar, I will never know. I miss you even before the plane takes off."

They shared a heartfelt kiss, and Jax walked through the security area and disappeared. Shannon trundled her suitcase toward the check-in point for her luggage with tears welling in her eyes. It sounded short, a month before she could see Jax again, but Shannon discovered that any time away from him was too long.

Chapter Sixteen

Shannon and Jax continued their cross-country romance, much to her family's amazement. Continued attempts to coerce Shannon into reconciling her differences with Andrew and giving their marriage another try did nothing to ease her pain at missing Jax. His absence in her life gave her mother hope that the romance would end, but Shannon was adamant that whatever happened with Jax, Andrew would not be a part of her life in the future. While her family didn't see any evidence of Jax, he and Shannon constantly texted each other and FaceTimed once a week. When she and Jax met in Adelaide, it felt like coming home, and she wondered how long she could hold her tongue and not blurt out that she loved him.

Seated at the pub, surrounded by her family, Shannon was surprised when a text message from Jax appeared. The message was short and to the point.

Can you talk?

Shannon responded, then moved away from the table, drawing a disapproving glare from her mother. The scowl did nothing to dim Shannon's anticipation, and she reasoned that if she had to accept Andrew's presence at the table, the least her mother could do was give her some slack if she was distracted by her phone. A moment later, she texted *yes, and* her phone rang.

"Hi, sweetheart. I know we didn't schedule this call, and I guess you are out with your family, but I wanted to revise our plan for next month."

Shannon's heart fell. Was he going to cancel?

"Ah, okay, what did you want to change?"

"Can you take a week's holiday? I was hoping you could come to the West to meet my family. They have heard so much about you that my mother ordered me to ask you to visit."

"Oh, you scared me for a minute. I thought you were going to cancel our visit."

"That's never likely to happen, but can you come? Even if we must delay it by a week or two, I want my family to meet my girl."

Jax and Shannon chatted for a while, making plans for the upcoming visit. When she returned to the table, her huge smile gave away the caller's name. Andrew was the first person to challenge her about taking calls during the meal.

"Don't you know it is rude to take a call in the middle of our meal?"

Shannon snorted. "Why didn't you know that fact when we were married? Your phone interrupted almost every meal we shared."

"That was different. My boss needed to contact me for critical business information. Your call was to flirt with your fancy man, and while you swoon over him here, who knows what he is doing on the other side of the country? Mark my words; the guy will ditch you when he tires of this cross-country affair, and if you wait too long, I might have moved on."

"Andrew, if you were the only man in the world, I still wouldn't want you. Do you attend these dinners to aggravate me? Because if that's the case, it's working."

The meal broke up shortly after, and Shannon walked out with her brother and his wife. Tammy grinned at Shannon and said. "We all know who the call was from, and even mentioning his name makes you smile, but what was so special this time?"

"Jax wants me to come to the West to meet his family this time. The flight is longer than to Adelaide so that I will need more days off. I should thank Andrew for being an ass because I have five years' worth of holidays to call on."

"Well, sis, things must be getting serious. Nobody invites their girlfriend or boyfriend to meet their parents unless things are serious."

"I think things were serious the first time we met, but he had separated from a cheating spouse, and so had I, so we needed to take things slowly. I'm excited and nervous to meet his family, but I guess I haven't got much to live up to, considering his first wife was cheating within the first month or two."

Shannon spent the next five weeks preparing for her trip to meet Jackson's family. After Andrew moved out and Shannon gained control of her finances, she purchased a few items of clothing. However, now that she would be away for a week, she decided that a shopping spree was in order. With her best friends a long drive away, Shannon asked Tammy to join her at the shops. Together, the girls replenished Shannon's depleted wardrobe, and after Tammy's insistence, Shannon purchased some racy lingerie.

"You know, we should book a spa day so that you are all smooth and lickable when you see your hunky boyfriend."

Shannon chuckled. She and Tammy got along fine, although, as Chris's wife, it would have been awkward if they had hated each other. Since her split with Andrew, Shannon and Tammy had become close. It felt good to have someone to confide in and someone to do girly things like shop and visit beauty parlours.

As the girls sat together at a café, Tammy asked the question that had run through Shannon's mind.

"If this is serious with your Jackson, where will you live if you and he become a committed couple?"

Shannon sighed. "From his comments, he and his family are close, whereas the more Mum tries to push Andrew's case for reconciliation, the less I want to see her. Moving to Western Australia would be an upheaval, but if meeting his family is his attempt to move us forward, then I would move. I would miss you and Chris, and I have work colleagues that I would miss, but I'd be glad to leave the whole mess of my failed marriage behind."

"I was lucky that Chris and I lived in the same area, but if I had the choice to stay with my family or move elsewhere with Chris, I would choose Chris every time. Making new friends and settling into a new environment is tricky, but I guess you did that when you moved away for college."

"I did, and even though I was excited about starting a different life, I was lucky that Amelia, Beck, and I became good friends. Camille kept telling me all these horror stories about sharing a house with others, but none of her dire warnings came to fruition."

"Your sister is a bit of a drama queen; I wouldn't take her advice. Although she has it pretty good, she pays no board and lives with your parents, free. Your mum cooks and does her laundry, and your dad keeps her car running. Chris tried convincing your parents they weren't doing Camille any favours by babying her, but Kathy didn't want to hear it."

"I'm glad I only had to stay with them briefly while looking to buy my house. Listening to Mum sprout Andrew's virtues made me crazy. Do you think she truly believes all that rubbish she spouts about forgiveness and reconciliation?"

Tammy laughed. "Kathy is delusional, and if I were you, I would have done him a serious injury long before the ratbag left."

Chapter Seventeen

When the plane touched down, Shannon let out a sigh of relief. Earlier in the day, when she had presented her ticket at the check-in desk, the receptionist raised her eyebrows at the readout but did not comment. As the business passengers loaded, the steward shook his head.

"We aren't loading economy passengers yet. You need to wait for us to call you."

Shannon looked at the ticket and blushed.

"Sorry, my boyfriend always books me in business class, and I didn't check the ticket."

Feeling embarrassed, Shannon sat with the ticket in her hands, wondering why Jax's assistant had booked the long-haul flight in an economy seat. Shannon wasn't so entitled that she couldn't travel economy, but after the many flights she had taken to visit Jax, this was the flight where she would have appreciated the extra space.

As she boarded from the back of the plane, it became apparent that Shannon had the worst seat in the aircraft. Her seat was in the last row against the plane's tail and outside the toilets. Her dismay showed, and the stewardess shrugged.

"Once the plane takes off, can I move seats?"

"I'm sorry, but there are no empty seats available. Whoever booked your flight must hate you because the purchaser chose this seat."

Shannon couldn't understand why Grace, Jax's assistant, had changed the booking from her previous flights. Passengers waiting in line for the conveniences leaned on her seat and crammed her already limited space. The flight was a nightmare as people filed back and forth, visiting the toilets. The only positive aspect of the flight was that she was at the back, and she deplaned while others waited their turn.

Trudging through the airport to the baggage collection carousel, Shannon fished for her phone, which had suddenly come to life. A text message from Jax said he was running late, but a driver would pick her up. She texted a thumbs up and waited until the carousel discharged her cases. Shannon's head ached, and all she wanted to do was find her driver and curl up on her bed at Jax's house. She scanned the people standing near the exit and, when she saw a sign with her name on it, headed for the man holding it. For a moment, she thought the driver was a joke, but it turned out his Hawaiian shirt, flip-flops, and beer belly were authentic, and this was her ride. Before she could refuse his assistance, the driver grabbed her bags, leaving her to follow behind. He threw her bags into the boot of a rusted sedan and opened the door for her. Shannon had little option but to slide onto the grubby seat and pray that this vehicle wreck would make it to Jax's flat without breaking down.

Shannon closed her eyes and massaged the pressure points on her temples. Soon, this nightmare would be over, and Shannon had every intention of kicking the assistant up the rear. The car pulled to a stop, and Shannon opened her eyes.

"What the hell is this? You were supposed to take me to my boyfriend's house."

The driver shrugged. "This address was the one the woman asked me to deliver you to, so if you have any complaints, you must take it up with someone else."

Shannon climbed out of the vehicle and stared in horror. The motel was a seedy-looking establishment, and Shannon had no doubts that someone was making mischief. The driver dropped her bags in front of the sign-in desk and disappeared without another word. A smirk crossed the face of the man working the desk.

"Sweetheart, unless you are a high-class hooker, you are in the wrong place. People don't stay here for holidays; most bookings are for an hour or two. You might want to get out of here before the punters begin to arrive and proposition you."

Tears welled in Shannon's eyes as she dialled Jax's number, which went to voicemail. Who knew how long it would take Jax to return her call? With little choice left, Shannon rang a taxi, and when the man arrived, she asked for a clean, economical motel recommendation. The ideal accommodation would be Jax's flat, but given her luck, she wouldn't be on his approved visitor list and would have to wait hours for him to arrive. Her arrival this time was less than welcome, and she hoped this disastrous day was not indicative of the week with Jax.

Shannon's night was only marginally better than the daytime drama. After she had a bath and ordered food, she tried to contact Jax again, but without success. What the hell was going on? She had flown from the other side of the country in the worst possible conditions, only to have him ignore her when she arrived. Shannon spent the night tossing and turning, trying to make sense of the welcome she had received. The disreputable driver, the wreck of a vehicle, the drop-off at a hooker hotel, and then the inability to contact Jax made Shannon's temper flare. Someone would pay dearly for this fiasco.

The directory in the foyer of Jax's building directed her to the fifth floor. Her eyes swept the expansive reception area, and Shannon walked to the woman behind the counter.

"Good morning, I am here to see Jackson Carruthers. Could you please let him know that Shannon is here?"

"Mr Carruthers is in a meeting. Would you like to come back in an hour or two?"

"Certainly not. I'll wait."

The receptionist looked nervous but said, "You can't wait here. We have a reputation to uphold, and people standing around with suitcases in tow is not the message we want to send."

"Fine, I won't wait."

The receptionist gave Shannon a smug grin and waited for her to leave. To the woman's amazement, Shannon left her bags on the floor and began opening office doors. She looked in each office and gave the occupants a friendly wave as she progressed to the next one. Shannon could hear the woman shouting, but continued her search. The last office door stood before her, and Shannon desperately hoped it was Jax's office because if it wasn't, she was sure the woman would have security remove her.

"Aha, I found you."

Jax's head shot up, and his mouth gaped in amazement.

"Shann, what are you doing here?"

"Um, spending a week to meet your family?"

"But that's not until next week."

"Could I please have a hug? I have had a horrific trip in more ways than one, and I think you need to fire whoever made the bookings for me."

Jax stepped forward and wrapped her in his arms. Shannon felt at peace for the first time since she boarded the plane. Jax's intercom beeped, and his assistant said,

"Mr Carruthers, your next appointment is here."

"Who is it?"

"Mr Myers from accounting."

"Tell Mr Myers I will reschedule, and you can clear my calendar for the day."

Jax kissed Shannon on the forehead and said. "Let's get out of here and see if we can sort out this mess."

Shannon and Jax reached his apartment thirty minutes later. They spent the time in the car catching up, but Shannon left her grievances until they were at his place. Once they arrived, Jax put Shannon's bags in his room and poured them a drink.

"Jax, that woman at reception isn't Grace, right?"

"No, Grace retired a month ago, but trained Brandi before she left."

"Well, either Grace is a lousy trainer, or your little receptionist is an evil bitch."

As Shannon relayed the previous day's events, Jax was slack-jawed at the trials Shannon had to endure.

"And now you tell me it is the wrong week?"

"God, how did she make such a mess of this week? Why didn't you call me when you first saw the driver and his vehicle?"

"Where is your phone?"

Jax fished through his pockets, which came up empty.

Shannon said, "I got a text message from your phone to say you would be running late, and when I tried to call you after that dreadful man left me at that hooker motel, I got your voicemail."

Jackson frowned. "I'm sorry to say you didn't talk to me. I was sure my phone was on the charger in my office, but I always take it with me when I leave. God, this is a mess. I've got a full week of meetings because Brandi said she cleared my calendar for next week."

Shannon deposited her drink on the side table and straddled Jax's knees. She ran her hands through his hair, and he tilted his chin, asking for a kiss. Their lips reunited in a sweet kiss, and Shannon teased Jax by nipping at his lips, but his patience ran out, and he gripped her head and took control of the kiss. The kiss was interrupted by Jax removing her shirt, and he resumed driving her into a frenzy with his lips as she unsnapped her bra and freed her breasts. Shannon unbuttoned Jax's shirt, baring the muscular torso she loved to touch. Shannon ground against Jax's growing erection and groaned at the feeling of him beneath her. Tomorrow might be uncertain, but Shannon intended to make the most of the evening.

Chapter Eighteen

Shannon groaned as Jax sat on the edge of the bed next to her. "Morning, sleepy head."

Shannon yawned and then grimaced at her perfectly attired bed partner.

"I'm tired because you kept waking me during the night."

Jax chuckled. "You'd better get some rest today because I intend to do the same thing tonight and every night of your visit. I'll leave my driver's number, and when you're ready to leave your bed, you can call him to take you wherever you want to go. I'll see what Brandi can do to free me up while you're here."

Shannon grinned. "Promises, promises."

Jax leaned over to kiss her and winked. "You should know by now I always keep my promises."

Shannon watched as Jax disappeared from view and then rolled from her bed. During the night, she came across an idea that might free Jax of the busy week she was sure his assistant had engineered, but her first job of the morning was to contact the airline, upgrade her tickets, and check the seating arrangement.

With her laptop open in front of her, Shannon pulled up the folder that held Grace's previous emails. As she scanned the contents, she finally found the first instalment, which included the mobile phone number Grace had included in the email. The tone of Grace's email was always friendly, so Shannon hoped the women would be able to help sort out the mess the assistant had made of her visit.

Shannon listened to the phone ring, her fingers crossed that it wouldn't go to voicemail. Just as she began to lose hope, a woman answered the phone.

"Hello, is this Grace? This is Shannon, Jax's girlfriend."

"Shannon, this is a lovely surprise. You sound just as I imagined you would."

Shannon laughed. "I was hoping you could meet me this morning to discuss a problem I'm trying to solve. You won't be breaking Jax's trust or sharing confidential information, but you are the best person to help me."

"I will help if I can. Why don't we meet at the coffee shop a block from Jackson's office? We can chat there."

An hour later, Shannon scanned the coffee shop, looking for the person who might be Grace. The clients numbered four: two men, a young mother with a baby in a stroller, and an older woman who waved at Shannon. With a grin, Shannon approached the table and returned the woman's hug. Once the women ordered their drinks, Shannon recounted the trials of her previous days.

"This morning, I upgraded the airline ticket and checked the seating, but I need help contacting the car service to deliver me to the airport and collect me at the other end. I also need your expertise in reorganising Jax's meetings and appointments to make time for us to spend together. When he arrived at the office, Jax rang me and said that his assistant was having trouble rescheduling his appointments. As you've worked there for years, I hope you will see what you can do. Spending a week filling in time waiting for Jax to return home from work does not fill me with glee, and he wanted me to meet his parents, which might be tricky if he has to work the whole time."

"Oh, dear me, I can't imagine what that girl was doing.'

"I have a feeling she thought she might have a chance with Jax if she took me out of the equation."

Grace stood. "Let's go and see if we can rectify the problem."

When Shannon and Grace stepped into the foyer, the shocked expression on Brandi's face amused Shannon.

"Brandi, we need to see Jackson, please."

The look on Grace's face made it clear that she could not prevent the women from seeing Jackson, so she buzzed him and announced his visitors. Jax rose from his seat to hug Grace and kiss Shannon's cheek.

"Two of my favourite ladies, and what a surprise to see you together. What brings you here, Grace?"

"If you send your assistant on an errand, I will reschedule as many appointments as possible. I need access to the computer for my files to book a car for Shannon to the airport here, and for a car to pick her up when she lands in Melbourne."

"I might send Brandi to HR. I don't need her here if she is incompetent enough to mix up flight bookings, car and delivery reservations, and cannot line up my week off with Shannon's arrival. She doesn't seem inept, but our mess suggests she is."

With Brandi out of the office, Grace quickly booked Shannon's transportation and provided the company's details in case her reservation needed to be changed. When Grace logged into Jackson's weekly planner, it became clear that she could reschedule most appointments and meetings. Grace postponed non-essential appointments and diverted the remaining items on Jax's calendar to his subordinates. Brandi returned as Grace reset Jackson's weekly planner, and seeing Grace at the computer, she charged into Jackson's office. Shannon and Grace exchanged pleased looks, and Grace said, "Maybe we should save Jackson from that woman's wrath. I doubt she will be here for more than the time it takes the HR people to discharge her services."

As Shannon opened the door of Jax's office, her brain refused to compute what she saw. Grace, however, was speedy in her response to the woman leaning over Jackson's desk with her breasts revealed.

"Goodness dear, put those plastic tits away; Jackson can see the real thing with Shannon, so he's not interested in your fake titties. Sexual harassment does not only go one way. You need to call past HR on your way out, and they will discharge you from employment here."

Brandi pulled up the neck of her shirt and stared at the three people in the office.

"You'll pay for ignoring me, Mr High and Mighty Carruthers and your tart will wish she hadn't ever met you."

The silence in the office after Brandi slammed the door was profound, and then the tension was relieved when Shannon laughed.

"Grace, I have to take my hat off to you. Your assessment of her plastic titties was hilarious. But Jax, my love, I have never seen a man back away from and look so repulsed by bare breasts."

"Yeah, well, I didn't know how to escape. If I walked around the desk towards the door, I feared Brandi would grab me, but there was no other avenue for escape. Thank God you came in when you did. Have a seat, ladies; averting a disaster calls for a drink."

When Jax and Shannon left that night, the weekly planner was empty, and Jackson turned the office running over to his second-in-command. She and Jackson had a few days to themselves before they travelled to Albany to meet with his parents.

Chapter Nineteen

Shannon was on edge as they pulled into the driveway of a home on the outskirts of Albany.

"Relax, sweetheart."

"What if they don't like me?"

"Shann, they will love you because I do. And let's face it, Marissa didn't set the bar too high."

Before Shannon could reply, the door burst open, and a mop-headed youngster ran towards the car.

"Uncle Jax, Uncle Jax, what took you so long? I've been waiting all morning."

Jackson alighted from the car with a smile, and the little girl launched herself at Jax. Shannon smiled at the warm reunion, and when she skirted the front of the vehicle, Jackson set the child down and introduced Shannon. The child clutched his hand, and Jax held out his other hand for Shannon. An older woman appeared in the opening as they approached the front door.

"Jackson, it's great to see you. Kelly, let Uncle Jackson go so I can hug him."

When the woman pulled from his embrace, she smiled at Shannon.

"You must be Shannon. Welcome to our home, dear. Jackson has kept you to himself; I feared he'd never introduce you because he was never good at sharing."

Shannon laughed. "It's good to meet you, Mrs Caruthers."

"None of that, Mrs Carruthers stuff; please call me Margie."

Shannon was soon engulfed in hugs and handshakes as they made their way through the house to the kitchen. The counters, loaded with platters of food, also held a variety of beverages.

"Let's get this food on the table before it gets cold."

The meal was cheerful, with people talking over one another and laughing at the quips Jax's brothers made. Any nerves Shannon had when they approached the house had dissipated during the chaos of the family's meal. Shannon answered the family's questions without hesitation when the focus turned to her. She sanitised the details of their first meeting, but for the most part, her answers were open and honest. Shannon knew that after Jax's first marriage, his family was looking out for him, and even though he attempted to stop the inquisition, his father failed to heed his warnings. Eventually, Jax said," Stop, Dad. Shannon is not Marissa. She doesn't care about my money, and she understands the word monogamy."

A tense silence fell over the table's occupants; Shannon felt uncomfortable with the direction of the questions but needed to reassure Mr Caruthers.

"I know you are trying to ensure that another scheming hussy is not conning Jax, but I love Jax. I have just come out of an unsatisfactory marriage, too, so we have been careful not to move too quickly with our relationship."

The gruff voice of his brother said, "If you and Jackson marry, would you sign a prenup?"

"Whoa, we aren't thinking of marriage as we are both legally wedded to our hateful spouses. But hypothetically, would I sign a prenuptial agreement if we were to get married? The answer is yes, I want Jax, not his money."

The awkward questions ended when Margie said, "Let's take our drinks onto the patio."

As the family collected their drinks, Jax turned Shannon to face him. He ran his knuckles along her cheek and tilted her head for a soft kiss.

"Are you alright? It never occurred to me that my family would interrogate you like a criminal under arrest."

"I'm not upset; they want to ensure I'm not a scheming hussie like your wife. I'd be surprised if they didn't have questions."

"I love you, Shannon Westcott."

Shannon smiled. "I'm glad because I love you too."

When Jackson's family were satisfied that Shannon was not threatening Jackson's well-being, they became friendly, and Shannon enjoyed the afternoon. Jackson's sister drew her to the side as they prepared to leave.

"I haven't seen Jackson so happy since before he met Marissa. Please don't hurt him; he looks like the sun and moon shine in your eyes, and if you do the wrong thing, I believe you have the power to destroy him."

"Dana, I have no intention of hurting Jackson. He, too, has the power to destroy me, and I have had enough pain in my previous relationship to last me forever."

Jackson approached his sister and gave her a warm hug. "Don't give my woman a hard time, Dana. I want my family to approve of Shannon, but even if you all disapprove, I intend to continue our relationship."

Dana hugged her brother. "I think she is lovely, and I am certain Mum and Dad do as well. I'm sure you can understand our concern considering the hussy you chose to marry, but your taste has improved with time."

Jackson grinned at his sister. "Thanks, sis; your approval means the world."

With her cases packed, Shannon was ready to leave for the airport, but after the enjoyable week she spent, she was reluctant to leave. She carried her suitcase into the living room; Jackson pointed to the couch and asked her to sit beside him.

"Shann, when my brother questioned you about us marrying, you said we weren't there yet, and I agree. I dislike how some couples announce their engagement before the divorce finalises, so I do not intend to buy you an engagement ring or even ask the question. But I don't want to put you on a plane and send you back home with no formal commitment to each other."

Shannon's eyes widened as Jax pulled a small ring box from his pocket.

"I bought you a promise ring. This ring will remind you that when we are free, I will ask the question, and hopefully, you will agree to marry me. Wear it on the ring finger on your right hand, and if you ever doubt me, look at the ring and believe in us."

Jax slid the small ruby ring onto Shannon's hand, and she glowed with her love for this man who started as a one-night stand.

"Thank you, Jax. I will treasure the ring, and whenever I look at it, I will remember how much you mean to me."

Chapter Twenty

Shannon coasted through the next few weeks, buoyed by Jackson's declaration that he loved her. The ruby ring glittered in the sunlight, and this physical reminder of his promise comforted her when she felt sad. Her days at work were busy as usual, and her Karate and running kept her active when she was so tired she wanted to climb into bed and hibernate. Slumped into her comfy armchair, the phone call from Jax surprised her.

"Hi, Jax. I'm too tired to do anything, but talking to you constantly revitalises me."

"Shan, something has happened, and I need to see you urgently. Can I visit tomorrow? I can catch an early flight and be there in the afternoon."

"Um, sure. Do you want me to pick you up?"

"No, I'll catch a cab to your place. See you soon."

The phone went dead as Jackson hung up, and his reserved attitude and abrupt ending of the call made Shannon nervous. What had happened that they couldn't wait until they met in two weeks? Shannon went through her bedtime ritual, but she still doubted that she would sleep well, even with the busy day ahead of her. Jackson's phone call made her nervous, and she was scared he had terrible news that would impact them. Shannon rubbed the ring on her finger as she lay in bed and remembered Jax's promise.

When Shannon finished work, she raced home to prepare for Jax's visit. She didn't know how long he would be staying, but she wanted to enjoy every moment of the unexpected visit. The knock on the door made her heart thump, and his defeated expression saddened her when she pulled the door open. Pulling him into a hug, Shannon held on until Jackson eased away from her. As he cupped her cheek, she caught the flash of his wedding ring and backed away with a distressed cry. Jackson's shoulders sagged, and he grabbed her hand and pulled her onto the couch next to him.

"Shann, remember the promise ring while I tell you what happened. About three days after you left, Marissa came to the office, declaring her undying love for me. I had security escort her out of the building. Every day for the rest of the week, she rang to apologise and beg me for another try; I declined and told her to stop ringing. When I received a call from her father, I knew she had pulled in the big guns. Her old man is one of the West's most influential men, both financially and politically. I knew he would apply pressure because he had gone out of his way to give Marissa whatever she wanted.

Even though I described what happened between Marissa and me and explained that she threw me out, he wouldn't listen. I told him I was in a serious relationship, and he told me to end it and reunite with Marissa, or he would use his influence to bankrupt me and ruin my reputation so nobody would deal with me. The bitch only wants me because that tart Brandi told her about you, but until I can move my business interests away from the West, I have no alternative but to comply."

Shannon wiped the tears from her eyes. "Are you living with her?"

"I'm living in the house, but I have a separate bedroom, and that's how it will stay until I can get rid of her for good."

"Dear God, what a mess. My mother is a pain, but your wife takes the cake. We can't see each other again until you sort this mess out."

"No."

"Well, Mr Carruthers, I have never slept with a man wearing another woman's wedding ring, and I have no intention of doing so. But I have a solution."

Shannon grabbed Jax's hand and slid the wedding band from his finger.

"There, now you are mine for tonight."

Unlike the previous night, after a separation, Jackson was in no hurry for their intimacy to end. He spent hours making love to Shannon and held her tight when they drifted off to sleep. His departure would be the hardest goodbye, and Shannon wept as he kissed her and left for the airport. Who knew how long it would take for Jax to reorganise his business so Marissa's father wouldn't destroy him? Shannon's mother's insistence that she give Andrew another chance paled in comparison to Marissa's father's threats. While her family could not force a reconciliation, Marissa's family had the social sway to ruin Jax if he did not comply with their wishes. Why would Marissa force Jax to resume their marriage when she didn't want the monogamy of a relationship before? Besides being a spoiled, spiteful bitch, did she have an alternative plan?

Shannon spent her days much as she did when she wasn't with Jax, but her sorrow made attending her karate classes and running with her friends on Saturday challenging. Shannon kept up her workload, but even the job with people suffering myriad injuries paled in comparison to the difficulty of not knowing when she might see Jax again. When her friend, Ben, suggested they get together for dinner after work, Shannon considered refusing. Still, Ben had been the person who gave her excellent advice earlier in her relationship with Jax, so she conceded.

The restaurant Ben chose was one Shannon had never been to, so there were no reminders of Jax at the venue. After choosing their meals, Ben said, "I have a proposition for you, but I can put that on the back burner if you want to tell me why you are so unhappy."

Shannon took a deep breath and spilled all the recent developments between her and Jax. It was freeing to tell someone who wouldn't try to blame her for being involved with a man who hadn't finalised his divorce or wanted to set her up with another man. When Shannon finished her explanation, Ben took her hand and tapped her ring.

"Why do you wear this ring? Is it from Jackson, and does it have significance?"

Shannon sniffed as she looked at the ring.

"It's a promise ring from Jax. It means he will ask me to marry him when we are free of our spouses."

"And do you believe him?"

"Yes, although it's hard when he's back living in the house with his wife. He says he isn't sharing a bedroom with her and tries to spend as much time as possible out of the house, but still, I worry."

"You need to hang in there. Your Jackson seems like a good bloke, and don't they say difficulties make success sweeter?"

"Okay, I'll keep the faith. What was the proposition you were going to make?"

"Ah, it's a professional proposal. You spend at least half your time assisting patients with mobility problems, mostly newly afflicted patients confined to wheelchairs. A mate and I want to see if we can develop an implant that sends the electrical pulses to the brain to help with movement."

"Wow. Where do I come in?"

"We'll use rats and other animals as testers, but eventually, we'll find people willing to undergo testing. That's where you come in: finding patients willing to test the device."

"I can do that, but I'd like to see how everything works before identifying patients to test."

"Great. You might be able to construct a checklist for people you identify as prospects so that we keep everything documented and above board."

Chapter Twenty-One

Random hearts, flowers, or smiling emojis appeared on Shannon's mobile, and as much as she wanted to respond, she guessed that Jax had contacted her when he was alone, and responding might make the situation worse if his wife caught him. After her conversation with Ben, Shannon kept a positive attitude, confident that Jax could sort out his business so they could be together.

Late one afternoon, an unknown number showed on her phone. Shannon hesitated before answering the phone, confident the unknown number was a telemarketer.

"Hello. Shannon, speaking."

"Shannon, hello. It's Margie Carruthers speaking. Jackson asked me to contact you because it is taking longer than he hoped to tie up his business interests here, and he is worried you will give up on him. How are you, dear?"

"Margie, it's good to hear from you. I must confess to being anxious that Jax is still living with his wife, and from what he has said about her, that situation is fraught with danger. But I have his promise ring, and when I start to doubt, I look at that and remember what it means."

"I understand your concerns. Marissa has Jackson tied down for the minute, but what is her motive? Who wants to live with a man who loathes you? But stick in there, dear. Jackson loves you, and even if it takes a while, he will make good on his promise."

The weekly dinner at the pub was a trial for Shannon, and she had long since given up trying to convince her mother that she and Andrew had no future. When Shannon arrived, Chris and Tammy were already seated, so she grabbed a drink and sat with them until the rest of her family came. Shannon had told Tammy and Chris what had happened between Jax and her, so when she sat, Tammy asked for any updates. Shannon shook her head and sighed. She told them that Margie Carruthers had called her at Jax's request and encouraged her to be patient.

The discussion between Shannon, Tammy, and Chris ended when the rest of her family arrived. Like a bad smell, Andrew arrived minutes after her family. His cocky smirk made Shannon feel uncomfortable. What did he have to smirk about? With a flourish, he pulled out his phone and punched in a few numbers before turning the screen towards her. The photo on the screen was of Jax and Marissa at a fundraiser. While Marissa clung to Jax with a predatory smile covering her face, Jax's smile was forced and didn't reach his eyes. Shannon closed her eyes, and when she opened them, Andrew flashed the phone so everyone at the table could see the photo. Tammy squeezed Shannon's hand, giving her sister-in-law a grateful smile.

"I told you that guy was cheating on you, and worse than that, he has left you dangling while he's reuniting with his ex. For goodness' sake, Shannon, end it with that bloke and return to me."

Shannon glared at Andrew. "Jax may have reunited with his wife, but you and I never will. Do I want to return to skrimping and saving while you and your mates spend money on beer, pizza and betting? Should I continue making you meals you never eat, just because there is always one little thing you need to finish at work? When you make it home for dinner, will you continue to walk away from the table the minute your phone rings? Will you schedule sex more than once a week? Will you leave the bedroom light on and use a position other than the missionary position? There is nothing that would convince me to return to you. You think you know what that picture tells you, but believe me, there is more to that than you will ever know."

"Dear, the photo proves that Jackson has reunited with his wife. You should reconsider Andrew's offer of a reconciliation."

"As my mother, I would have thought you wanted me to be happy. I was unhappy from the beginning of our marriage; the longer it dragged on, the worse it got. I have repeatedly described what happened in our marriage, and you seem to have a mental block. When you were first married, would you have been happy having sex once a week in a dark bedroom? Would you have been happy if Dad had arrived home hours late most nights, and would you have been happy if Dad had constantly answered the phone during your meal? If you answered yes to any of those questions, I feel sorry for you. Even if Jax and I don't reconnect, he's shown me what it's like to be loved. He's kind, funny, intelligent and sexy, and I will not settle for less."

Shannon's parents watched as Shannon walked away. Shannon's sister Camille said, "Why do you do that, Mum? I have heard Shannon tell you how horrible her marriage was numerous times, and you sweep her explanations away as though they are unimportant. No one knows what happens inside a marriage. Still, in Shannon and Andrew's case, we have had explicit knowledge about the unhappiness Shannon experienced. I notice that Andrew doesn't call her out on her accusations, which is telling in itself. For goodness' sake, leave her alone."

Shannon did not hear her sister's defence of her, but if she knew her sister believed her, it would have cheered her. The photo that Andrew flashed at her made Shannon's heart hurt. Anyone who knew Jax would have seen the despair and unhappiness in the image, and even though he wasn't here to calm her, Shannon knew that Jax wasn't cheating. He hadn't been able to disengage himself from the toxic relationship, and even though it hurt to see his unhappiness, Shannon knew she had to be patient.

A week later, as Shannon left work, her phone chimed. She continued walking as she slid the screen down to read the text. Her feet stopped as though they were stuck in the pavement when Shannon realised the message was from Jackson. He asked to see her over the weekend, and his assistant would email her plane ticket and driver information if she agreed. Their meeting was to be in Adelaide, but he needed to see her because he had some distressing news. While Shannon was excited about seeing Jax, his unfortunate news played on her mind. What more could go wrong? Had the universe decided she and Jax didn't deserve to be together?

Chapter Twenty-Two

When the plane touched down, Shannon's emotions wavered between excitement and dread; whatever Jax wanted to tell her must be urgent and vital, and that thought brought neither comfort nor assurance. With no luggage to collect from the carousel, Shannon hefted her carry-on bag and scanned the area for her ride. A man in a suit held a sign with her name, so she made her way through the crowd.

"Hi, I'm Shannon Wescott."

The man smiled. "And I'm your ride. Do you want me to carry your bag?"

"No, there are only a few changes of clothes, so it's fine."

Shannon and her driver chatted about the weather and other inconsequential things until the car pulled up in front of the Ferns Motel. Her check-in took a few minutes because she wasn't sure if Jax had booked the room in her name or his. When the receptionist found the booking, it was in Jax's name, and she wouldn't tell Shannon which room he was in.

"For goodness' sake, ring Mr Carruthers and tell him I've arrived."

"This is highly improper. I'm certain Mr Carruthers didn't want to be interrupted."

"And I'm certain if you don't make the call, Jackson and I will give you horrific reviews, and you won't even be able to entice the homeless folk to live here."

"What is the problem, Miss?"

"Your receptionist won't ring to check that I am here to meet Jackson Carruthers."

"Sandy, make the call. If Miss Westcott is here to meet Mr Carruthers, he will be displeased that we stopped her from seeing him."

Minutes after the woman made the call, the lift landed on the ground floor, and Jax walked out. He walked towards her, and she dropped her bag and flung herself into his arms. Jax pushed the hair away from her face and cupped her cheeks.

"It's so good to see you. Let's grab your bag and get out of here."

When they reached his room, Shannon said, "I don't want to hear your bad news yet. Please leave it for now; I've missed you so much. All I want to do is climb into bed with you. The bad news can wait a while."

Jax pulled her close and kissed her. Shannon felt like she was burning up; her desire to be with Jax was so strong that it almost knocked her off her feet.

"Please, Jax, I need you."

With efficient moves, Jax removed his shirt and undid his pants. Shannon couldn't decide whether she wanted to undress or watch Jackson disrobe. His raised eyebrows at her lack of action made her decision for her, and she quickly stripped off her clothes. They landed on the bed with a tangle of limbs, and the only sounds were their quickened breaths and throaty moans. Once their urgent need was satisfied, Jax spent the next hour ensuring no part of Shannon went untasted or unloved. Shannon's emotions boiled over, and knowing it could be a long time until they could be together again, she snuggled closely when their passion subsided.

"Okay, do you want to tell me your bad news?"

"I think we'd better get dressed, and I'll order room service before I do."

The meal Jax ordered arrived swiftly, and while they ate, they caught up on the time they had apart. Shannon thanked him for asking his mother to check on her, and the conversation reassured her that Jax was doing all he could to unravel the problem of his unwanted wife.

"Yeah, Mum and Dad have been supportive, and Dad even sought legal advice to see if we could force Marissa and her father to cease because what they are doing is blackmail. But then another complication arose."

"And now you are in knots trying to find a way to tell me that won't crush my hopes."

Jax dropped his head, his eyes fixed on his hands.

"Yes. You know that I'm living in the same house as Marissa?"

"Yes."

"My bedroom is at the opposite end of the house to hers. Most nights, you come to me in my dreams, even if I work until I'm exhausted. I miss you so much that I welcome those dreams because at least I can imagine being with you. The night in question, I was asleep, dreaming of you. It felt so real; you were riding me, and I gripped your hips to drive into you deeper when I realised it wasn't a dream. I came before I could push her away, and clearly, I wasn't wearing a condom. I pushed her off, raced to the bathroom, and threw up until my stomach was empty. She entered the bathroom as I sat on the floor, dry-retching and laughed."

Jax looked up at Shannon; the tears in her eyes broke his heart. He shook his head before he spoke again.

"I had a test for STDs, and the doctor gave me some precautionary antibiotics. I finished those, and the doctor tested me again; I'm clear, but there's a problem. That incident happened about six weeks ago, and I didn't want to tell you in case you ditched me. Selfish, I know, but Shann, the only thing that gets me through the days is thinking about us together."

"Let me guess; the slag is pregnant, isn't she?"

Jax's shoulders dropped, and tears welled in his eyes.

"Yes."

Shannon walked to the mini bar, pulled out two drinks and handed one to Jax before she downed the other.

"So, what happens now?"

"She swears the baby is mine, although that is questionable considering the number of blokes she hooks up with. However, if that is the case, I will apply for sole custody. Will you still want me if I am a single parent?"

Shannon clasped his hand. "The only time I will walk away from you is if you tell me you no longer love me."

"I don't know when I can see you again. If Marissa thinks I'm still seeing you, she will whine at her father, and he will act on his revenge plan. I know I should call their bluff, but what kind of life can I give you if I'm broke and my reputation is in shreds?"

"I must say I'm disappointed at this new problem, but surely she can't cause any more problems. When that photo of you and Marissa at a charity function popped up on Facebook, Andrew shared it gleefully, thinking he would shock me into reuniting with him. All I saw in that image was her victorious smile and the pain and hurt in your eyes. It didn't matter that you had plastered a smile; your eyes told the truth, and I felt like weeping."

"Is that fool still trying to get you to restart your marriage?"

"Yes, and so is my mother. I told her off again, but I don't intend to eat many more meals with them if she can't stop pressing. I wonder what my father thinks; he never says anything, but then again, he never tells Mum to stop hassling me."

The following morning, when Jax left the motel room, Shannon wrapped herself in the bedding that smelled like him and cried. She hoped that she would regain some composure before she had to fly out at midday.

Chapter Twenty-Three

"Shannon, when you finish with that patient, can you meet me in my office?"

Shannon looked up at her boss and nodded. She wondered what her boss wanted as she underwent the exercises her patient needed to complete the following week. Greg Harvey, the head of allied services, was a man Shannon had little time for. She thought he was pompous and a know-it-all, and considering he had no experience in physiotherapy, he had no right to question her treatments. This meeting interfered with her schedule, but he thought himself so important that she would have to stay later tonight to catch up while he was swilling his sixth or seventh beer.

After knocking, Shannon pushed the door open and was surprised to find Ben seated in a chair. Shannon looked at Greg Harvey, confused.

"I'm sorry; obviously, I'm too early."

"No, no, I wanted to tell you and Ben of a wonderful opportunity a benefactor has offered us. Many people in the medical field know you are working on a device to send signals to the spine, and it's come to the attention of a generous woman."

"And what does that mean for Shannon and me?"

"Ben, you will have added resources to pursue your goals."

Shannon frowned. "Will this person have any control over our project?"

"I think she will be too busy, considering she has recently started her business funding medical research. You two and I are invited to a gala evening where Mrs Cruthers will announce the recipients of the grants."

Shannon jumped to her feet. "What is Mrs Carruthers's first name?"

"Ah, let me look. Her name is Marissa."

Shannon felt the room tilt and held onto the desk until Ben placed his hand on hers and led her back to a chair.

"Mr Harvey, Marissa Carruthers is a cruel, vindictive woman who will have invited Ben and me to humiliate me. She will not fund our project, and since she is handing out her father's money, I see no reason why we should play along with her."

"You know this woman?"

"By reputation, and I have no wish to meet her face to face. Please attend her gala if you believe this is legitimate, but I will decline to attend. Thank you."

"If you want your job, you will accompany Ben and me to this gala. Hospitals always need more money, and we will be there if she has cash."

"Please, Mr Harvey, my presence will not encourage her to fund our research. She will take pleasure in humiliating me, and we won't be on the receiving end of any cash outlay."

"Miss Wescott, let me repeat myself. If you want your job, you will be there."

When Ben and Shannon left the director's office, they were silent as they walked through the corridors.

"Cancel your last appointments and meet me in the break room in fifteen minutes. We need to devise a strategy."

Shannon nodded blankly and entered her office. Shannon retraced her steps after a few minutes of conversation with her admin officer. As she waited for Ben to arrive, Shannon sat in numb disbelief. How could the foul woman get her claws into Shannon and Ben's research?

Shannon knew this invitation and offer of funds was an elaborate scam to humiliate her.

Ben entered the breakroom fifteen minutes later and flicked the kettle on before taking a seat.

"I trust what you're saying, but how do we escape the dinner but still retain our jobs? And what kind of stunts might she pull to humiliate you?"

"Greg Harvey is a prat. We wouldn't be in this position if he had listened to what I'm saying. I'm unsure what she will do because she doesn't want to get involved in something that could have a negative impact on her. Maybe I should call Jackson and ask if he is accompanying her. His arrival will blindside me if I'm not expecting to see him."

"I'll leave you to contact your beau, but try to devise a plan that helps."

Shannon watched Ben leave, and after a moment's hesitation, she pulled out her phone and dialled. As the phone rang, Shannon tapped her nails on the counter. What if Jax had deleted her details and refused to take a call from her for fear that his wife would make life even more difficult? Shannon had given up hope when Jax answered.

"Hold on, please."

Shannon could hear Jax talking to someone and the sound of his footsteps as he walked away from his colleagues. She listened to the sound of a door closing, and the voice she wanted to hear said, "Sweetheart, this call is a surprise. Is there a problem?"

As Shannon poured out the details, she heard Jax groan.

"Damnation, I had no idea she intended to include you and your colleague in this farce she is perpetuating. I'm sorry your job and friend have become embroiled in her nasty game. We could pretend we don't know each other, but I think that boat has sailed if she has invited you. Even if the night is tough, she has given us a present so we can see each other. The hard part will be keeping my hands to myself."

When she and Jax disconnected, Shannon felt a sense of despair overwhelm her. What had she done in her previous life that she had to atone for?

Chapter Twenty-Four

Ben and Shannon entered the conference centre and, after taking a drink from one of the circulating servers, made their way through the crowd, chatting to associates and acquaintances from the health sector. Ben leaned forward and whispered, "Do you see either of them?"

Shannon shook her head and smiled. "Maybe they had a flat tyre, and they'll be running late."

Shannon still hadn't spotted Jax or Marissa when the servers announced dinner. From the tables they passed, they saw name tags for the guests, and as the tables began to fill, it became clear there was no place for either of them to sit. Moving to the back of the hall, Ben said, "Round one to the wicked witch. Do you want to leave and try explaining to Greg Harvey that there was a mix-up with the guest list and we weren't on it?"

"Please take your seat so we can serve the meal."

Shannon glared at the officious server and said, "Please show us to our places, sir. We can't see any vacant seats."

The server looked towards the table and frantically scanned the seating arrangements. When the man's face paled, Shannon knew he had realised that the seating arrangement was two places short.

"Don't worry, mate. My companion and I will leave, but please find Mr Greg Harvey and inform him that we weren't on the dinner list."

"Oh, no, no. That won't do. Please give me a minute while I prepare another table."

As the food began to fill tables and the noise level dropped as people concentrated on their meals, Ben and Shannon sat at the back of the room. While the server had managed to find another table, there were no extra meals. Shannon's tummy rumbled, and she muttered, "This night is not only going to be unpleasant, but I may die of starvation before it ends."

"Never fear; Menulog is here."

Shannon had her first view of Marissa when the woman approached the stage to welcome her guests. As she began to speak, a loud knock on the entry door halted her in her tracks. As Ben retrieved the large pizza box from the delivery driver, Marissa glared at him. Never one to cower, Ben said, "Don't mind us. Your organiser can't count, and rather than disturbing your event with our rumbling tummies, we've ordered food. We'll munch on our pizza while you give your little welcome speech."

Shannon ducked her head, trying to hide her giggles. God, she loved how fearless Ben could be when the situation called for it. Some of the guests looked amused, but Marissa looked furious. Ben leaned towards Shannon. "Round two to us."

When the diners finished their meals, Marrissa urged them to mingle and enjoy some excellent wines. Shannon quickly lost patience as she watched Marissa drag Jax around the room, chatting with other healthcare professionals, and she avoided contacting Ben or her. While desperate to speak to Jax, she knew she couldn't risk it for fear of giving herself away.

"I like your taste in men. If I weren't happily married, I might try my luck."

Shannon laughed. "Trust me, my friend; he doesn't bat for your team."

They were laughing together when a voice cut in.

"I'm glad to see everyone is enjoying my largesse. I suspect your lower-paid jobs in the medical profession don't allow you to mix with the top executives."

Ben straightened, glaring at the woman who slung the first barb.

"Mrs Caruthers, perhaps we should start with introductions rather than jibes. I'm Doctor Ben Radcliff, resident surgeon at Holsworth Hospital, and my colleague is…"

"Don't bother; I know who she is."

As she tucked her arm through Jax's arm, Marissa said, "I believe you know my husband. I thought you would be happy to see each other."

Shannon looked at Jax and smiled. "It's good to see you, Jax."

Shannon looked at the woman and shook her head.

"Our medical director ordered Ben and me to attend your presentation to secure funding for the device Ben and I are working on. I tried to convince him that you wouldn't grant us funds, but he is too damn stubborn for his own good."

"I had no intention of donating money to you. I wanted to see what kind of woman would have an affair with a married man. The medical profession should drum out a hussy like you. Tonight, you're parading around with your doctor friend on your arm. Do you sleep with your patients and random men like my husband?"

The conversation had grown heated, and other guests became aware of the slights and insults.

Ben gripped Shannon's hand and squeezed. It was his signal to leave, but Shannon had a slight or two to aim at the woman.

"I met your husband when you were separated, but I hardly think you can question my morals when you fuck any man with a pulse. And even though your long-suffering husband is here, it didn't stop you from screwing the blond waiter behind the dividing curtain earlier tonight. I'm glad you don't intend to offer us a grant; Ben and I wouldn't want an association with you to sully our research."

As the woman gasped, Shannon placed her hand on Jax's arm.

"I'm sorry you are married to a cow like her."

She leaned up and kissed his cheek, and then she walked out. Jax wrenched his arm away from Marissa and headed to the bar.

Greg Harvey had heard the tail end of the argument and couldn't grovel enough, hoping to get in Marissa's good books. She clarified that she would fund the project if Shannon were no longer involved. In disgust, Ben stepped away from the woman.

"There is no project without Shannon."

Marissa shrugged. "Well, there is no money while that woman works at the hospital."

Ben shrugged. "A benefactor with a malicious hidden agenda, how novel."

When Ben exited the building, he scanned the area for Shannon as he walked to his car. He stopped short when Jax stepped out of the laneway behind the building. The two men propped and regarded each other.

"Are you and Shannon together? Are you dating her?"

Ben laughed. "No, I am not dating her. Even though Shannon is attractive, you are more my type."

It took a moment for Ben's comment to register, and when it did, Jax laughed.

"Sorry, but you're not my type. Can you give me a minute alone with Shann?"

"Sure, but don't take too long, or that witch you are married to will send someone to find you. We've had enough unpleasantness tonight to last a lifetime."

Jax walked towards Shannon as she stood next to Ben's car.

"Jax, I'm sorry. She made me angry, and I couldn't let her comments go unanswered."

"We only have a few minutes, and I won't waste them discussing that baggage."

Jax hooked his hands around Shannon's waist and pulled her against him. The kiss was sweet and loving, but Shannon didn't want sweet, and she grabbed the lapels of his jacket and deepened the kiss. Jax groaned as Shannon tested his self-control, and when he pulled back, they were both panting.

"Shann, I love you so much that this whole marriage shit is torture."

Shannon rested her head against his heart.

"All that keeps me going is my memories and your ring. Hopefully, when she gives birth, you will be free and clear. If she wants a functioning offspring, she might want to stop drinking. Hasn't she heard of fetal alcohol syndrome?'

"I've tried to stop her, but she won't listen."

Ben stood next to the couple, still in each other's arms.

"Sorry to break this up, but the longer you're out here, " he glanced at Jax, " the more likely someone will see you, and Shannon's reputation is already in the toilet from that bitch's comments. I feel your pain, man, but I promise to look out for your woman until you can do it yourself."

Jax and Ben shook hands, and then Jax walked away as Shannon's tears started to fall.

"Come on, sweetheart. Let's get you home and away from that vindictive bitch."

Chapter Twenty-Five

"What do you mean you are ending my contract?"

"After your disgusting comments to a prospective benefactor, the hospital administration isn't willing to forego a large donation because you are on staff. Mrs Caruthers has pledged one hundred thousand dollars to the hospital, but only if you are no longer employed here."

"I told you when the invitation came that the woman only wanted to humiliate me and wasn't likely to fund the work Ben and I are doing. But did you listen? Of course not, because you never listen to advice from others."

"Your comments only dig your grave deeper, Miss Westcott."

"How much worse can the situation get?"

"Mrs Caruthers has far-reaching influence. If you continue your criticisms, you might discover how much worse things can get. Pack your belongings; security will be along shortly to escort you from the building."

Stunned, Shannon left the man's office and walked to her desk in the Allied Health Department. Did the man believe she should have taken the insults and slurs with a smile pasted on her face? Shannon left a message for Ben to call her and stacked her belongings on her desk. When Security arrived, an apologetic man handed her a cardboard box, and Shannon packed her belongings away before following him from the building. Before exiting for the last time, she gave her security pass and identity card to her escort and walked away from the building that had been her workplace for seven years.

Despite numerous applications to hospitals around the area, no one was willing to hire Shannon. Frustrated, Shannon went to the HR department at the large hospital that had rejected her for the vacant Physio position. The embarrassed manager shrugged when Shannon asked why she wasn't a good fit for the role.

"I'm sorry, Miss Wescott, but hospitals running for a donation from the Carruthers Foundation have been warned not to hire you if they want to have their application considered. I realise it smacks of bias, and the rejections don't reflect your suitability for the jobs you've applied for. However, considering that most hospital budgets are limited, we must do everything possible to secure additional funding. I doubt you will find a position in any hospital, hoping for the donation."

Shannon left the building feeling desperate. How could she afford to live without a job? Would Shannon have to apply at fast-food places to flip burgers or fry chips? Even though she no longer worked at the hospital, Greg Harvey could not prevent her from meeting her former colleagues at the pub. While her former colleagues sympathised with her situation, few had suggestions for overcoming the ban. Lisel, the other physio, suggested that if the hospitals were unwilling to hire her, aged care facilities would always be looking for staff. The pay gap would be comprehensive, but surely it was better than fast food? Shannon tucked that suggestion away in her brain as she enjoyed her night out with her friends.

Shannon sat facing Mrs Jordan, the woman who held her job prospects in her hands. An age-card facility was not what she had trained for, but with her medical experience, surely she could adapt to a different environment.

"Miss Wescott, thank you for your application, but you are too well qualified for the vacant position."

Shannon's shoulders slumped.

"Why would you apply here and not at another hospital? I'm unsure as to the reasons for your dismissal from the hospital that you've been working at for seven years, and I'm confused as to why you didn't line up a new job before you finished at your last post."

Shannon considered spinning a yarn but decided the truth would be best.

"After my divorce, I met a man in Perth, and after spending five days with him, I went home. He and I had separated from our spouses, but I never imagined more would come of our meeting. He came to Melbourne to find me, and our relationship grew. We would meet once a month in Adelaide, and when he asked me to come to Perth to meet his family, I knew he was serious."

As Shannon continued her story, Mrs Jordan shook her head in amazement. When she finished, Shannon looked at the woman.

"You are my last chance at securing a job. I know I'm overqualified, but besides the jobs most carers provide, I might be able to add extra with my physio experience. My other options are at fast food restaurants or cafe waitressing jobs."

"Can't your beau help you out?"

"If the baby is his, Jax wants to sue for sole custody and seeing me muddies the water."

Mrs Jordan tapped her fingers on the desktop and then said,

"I will give you a three-month trial. I will terminate your employment if I hear of misdemeanours or you lording it over the other carers because of your qualifications."

"Thank you so much. You won't regret your decision."

Chapter Twenty-Six

Shannon closed down her computer and sighed with satisfaction. Despite her unorthodox beginning at the centre, Shannon had effortlessly fit into the roster and procedures. Compiling data from the newly introduced programs at the centre kept her busy during her breaks, but if she were to convince other centres to implement some of them, she would need to prove their worth.

After learning the other carers' skills and the centre's running schedule, Shannon asked for permission to use her physio skills and work with some of the more mobile residents. The program, which began with ten residents, had blossomed, and even those who used wheelchairs participated in some exercises. The first thing Shannon noticed during her three-month trial was that the carers were run off their feet, and many of the residents were sitting in chairs in front of the television with vacant expressions. These people who had been parents and guardians holding down paying jobs were discarded, thrown on the scrap heap, waiting patiently to die. There had to be more to life than this.

After much consultation and planning, the centre now boasted raised vegetable gardens that residents could tend, and the cook used the produce in their meals. Some ladies wanted access to the kitchen to bake cakes and cookies. So, instead of buying biscuits in plastic containers, Mrs Jacobs used the money to purchase the ingredients for the ladies to bake biscuits and cakes for morning and afternoon tea.

Shannon tracked the residents' mobility and gradually introduced skills they thought they had lost. With people more motivated,

Shannon encouraged families to see their parents and relatives more often. Some grandparents watched their grandchildren playing sports, and another group participated in the local lawn bowls competition. She didn't want families to have tea and then leave; instead, she wanted them to collect their parents when grocery shopping or picking up the kids from school. The centre's activities were everyday excursions that residents had carried out as parents and guardians for many years.

As Shannon prepared to leave, Mrs Jacobs entered the break room, where she collated her data.

"Well, Shannon Westcott, I never imagined hiring you would send my orderly centre into a whirlwind of activity. And I must say, it was the best decision I ever made. The skills you've reintroduced to a cohort of previously inactive citizens have rejuvenated many residents. The cooking ladies set up morning and afternoon tea, and the fresh produce available at the back door has encouraged the chief to be more adventurous. The other carers have less to do as some of the ladies are making their beds and helping others. I worry, though. You spend so much time here that you can't have a life outside the centre. Have you heard from your beau?"

Shannon forced a smile. "I spend time here because I enjoy what I do and am thrilled at how the residents have accepted the challenge to live their lives instead of sitting in front of the tellie and waiting to die. I get emojis from Jax most weeks, but I'm unclear about how the pregnancy is going and how soon we can be together."

"Are you sure the man is not stringing you along? I'd hate to see you get hurt."

"Many months ago, before his horrid wife got her father involved in the breakdown of their marriage, he gave me this ring. Jax called it a promise ring, and the pledge was that he would propose as soon as we were both free of our marriages. It keeps me grounded and gives me hope."

Jackson parked in the circular driveway and alighted from the car with a grim expression. Marissa laughed off his concerns when he tried to convince her to stop drinking for the baby's sake. Jax couldn't decide what else he could do if his conversation with her parents didn't prove worthwhile. A butler opened the door and stepped back to allow Jax to enter. He had notified Leo Bossinelli that he would call after work and requested that Maria Bossinelli be present as well. When the butler showed him into the sitting room, Jax internally scoffed at the ostentatious show of wealth on display in the room. Any wonder Marissa was spoiled rotten?

Leo stood and offered his hand to Jax with a show of good humour and approachability. While shaking the man's hand was the last thing Jax wanted to do, he knew that he needed to keep his agitation hidden because, at any show of nerves, the man was like a shark that smelled blood in the water. Jax declined the offered drink, and when everyone settled, Jax began.

"Leo, you and Maria know I want to finish the farce of a marriage Marissa and I are living. She has not stopped bed-hopping, and I can't understand why you pander to her when you know our marriage is a sham. She does not want to be married to me; she wants to prevent me from moving on with the woman I love, and the longer this marriage fiasco drags on, the more damage she does to having friendly relations when the baby is born."

Leo Bossinelli steepled his fingers and scrutinised his son-in-law. Jax didn't shirk from his father-in-law's inspection, but his hope died at the man's impassive face.

"Jackson, you seem man enough to me to satisfy a woman. Maybe you need to try a little harder."

"Leo, when we married, I didn't know that Marissa didn't understand the term monogamy or when she said the words forsaking all others until death do us part, she didn't understand what she was saying. Within months of the wedding, she announced she wanted an open marriage, which was never acceptable to me, so she threw me out. Please end my suffering and release me from the agreement."

"Sorry, Jackson, but Marissa tells me she loves you, and if you join her in bed, she will stop her wayward behaviour."

"It seems we are at a stalemate because I will never again join her in her bed. Even if I loved her, which I don't, I wouldn't bed her for fear of infection. The number of men she has bedded since our marriage must number in the hundreds, and I'm surprised she isn't suffering from a nasty STD."

Jax watched for a response from either Leo or Maria, but their facial expressions didn't change. With a sigh, he raised his second concern.

"I have another worry, and it regards your future grandchild. Health experts have proven that alcohol during pregnancy harms the unborn baby. Marissa drinks to excess, and every drink causes more damage. I hoped you might convince her to enter a detox unit so she stays sober for the remainder of her pregnancy."

Maria spoke for the first time. "Don't be absurd, Jackson. I drank when I was pregnant with Mariss, and she is unaffected."

"Good Lord, son, it never occurred to me that you were a wowser. What harm can it do for Marissa to have a drink or two?" Leo shook his head to show his disappointment in Jackson.

Jackson wanted to shout at these two oblivious parents.

"Maria, Leo, your daughter doesn't have a drink or two. She is a borderline alcoholic. She reties every night, reeling and stumbling along the hallway, and rises every morning with a hangover. There is a thing called fetal alcohol syndrome, which is damage caused by excessive drinking during pregnancy. When your grandchild is born brain-damaged or physically impaired, I can say I told you so, but what of the poor damned infant? He or she will need lifelong support; I hope you are ready to provide that support. Why don't you visit early one morning? If you don't warn Marissa about your visit, you will see what I'm saying is true. Whatever you do, Leo, don't plan for the child to take over your business when you retire; it will be lucky if it can tie its shoelaces."

Jax had failed. Shaking his head at how obtuse his in-laws were, Jax quit their house. He couldn't convince the Bossinelli parents of the futility of his marriage and the danger to the baby. The only person who could ease his mind was Shannon, and although his wife monitored his calls, he intended to ring her whenever he wanted.

If his wife could fuck random strangers, he could call the woman he loved.

Chapter Twenty-Seven

The phone call from Jax surprised Shannon because she thought he was trying to keep his distance, making it easier to apply for sole custody of the baby if it was indeed his child. While his call came as welcome proof that Jax still loved her, Shannon's heart went out to him because he sounded sad and defeated. How much longer could this madness go on? Marissa's pregnancy seemed to drag on and on, and even one day more seemed too long.

Shannon's job and her program development for other centres to access kept her busy, but Jax's call prompted her to ring his mother, Margie, to see if the family could help.

"Hello, Margie? This is Shannon."

"Shannon, dear, it is lovely to hear from you. Are you calling for a particular reason or just catching up?"

"For a particular reason. Jax called me a few days ago, sounding defeated and sad. I would fly over, but I think my presence would exacerbate the situation, and I hoped you could persuade him to take time off and spend time with his family. This damn pregnancy seems endless for me, but for Jax, living with that tart must make each day miserable."

Shannon heard Margie sigh. "It breaks my heart to think of what Jackson and you are going through. That woman doesn't want to marry Jackson, and her father uses his business influence to blackmail him. I know he is waiting for the child to be born because he believes Marissa's father will have to relent when the child is not his. He is also concerned about the baby's welfare, considering the woman drinks like a fish."

"From here, I can do nothing except commiserate on the phone, but maybe you can talk him into coming home?"

"I will ring him and suggest he come home for a break. Thank you for the suggestion."

Jackson didn't call again, and Shannon wondered if she had overstepped the mark by ringing his mother. Hopefully, he didn't consider her concern for his health as interfering, but in his frame of mind, who could tell?

Jax had spent as much time as possible away from the house he and Marissa lived in, but as her due date came closer, he felt it was his responsibility to get the stubborn woman to the hospital. They had argued about a home birth, and unbeknownst to Marissa, Jackson had booked her into the maternity section of the general hospital. While he was sure Marissa would come out of the birthing process without complications, he wasn't sure the baby would fare as well. Jackson hoped that by the time Marissa went into labour, she would be in too much pain to argue about where she gave birth.

The wailing and cursing that greeted Jackson as he returned home one evening was the most welcome sound he had heard in quite some time. If he was correct, Marissa was in labour. Making his way towards the section of the house where she lived, Jackson began to time the wails and moans. When he pushed the door, the sight of his sweaty, red-faced wife clutching her belly greeted him.

"How long have you had the pains?"

"What the hell do you care?"

"Okay, you wanted a home birth, so I'll leave you to it."

When Jackson reached the door, Marissa screamed, "No, don't leave me."

"Give me a minute to get a wet cloth."

Jackson had every intention of calling the ambulance. Taking Marissa by surprise was the only sure way to get her to concede defeat and allow the paramedics to load her into the ambulance. After making the call, he returned to the bedroom and laid the wet cloth on Marissa's forehead.

As the nurses settled Marissa into the birthing suite, Jackson slipped out to ring her parents. Once he made the call, Jackson sat in the waiting room, and the temptation to ring Shannon was strong, but at the moment, what could he tell her apart from the fact that Marissa was in labour? Before he could succumb to the temptation, a nurse called to him.

"Mr Caruthers, your wife is calling for you."

Jackson grimaced. Marissa intended to make him see this farce to the bitter end, and his presence wasn't so much to comfort her as to punish him for walking away from their toxic marriage. Marissa writhed and groaned in the birthing suite as Jax used a damp cloth on her forehead and held her hand. The time slipped by, and as Jax watched Marissa struggle with the pain and birthing process, he wondered why women continued to have babies. Jackson couldn't fathom how women returned for a second and third child when they knew what had to happen to birth the baby after nine months of discomfort. When the doctor told Marissa to push, he smiled and instructed her to give one more push, and the baby would be born.

The squalling, red-faced infant slipped into the world, and Jackson closed his eyes. The baby's curly black hair and its ebony skin put paid to Marissa's claim that the baby was his, but his fear that the baby would suffer from her excessive drinking seemed to have come to fruition. The baby screamed and fussed as the nurses attempted to clean the little boy. No patting or bouncing settled the baby, and Jax stood to take the child from the nurse.

"My wife is an alcoholic who refused to stop drinking even when I explained the damage she was doing to the baby. It is six or seven hours since my wife had alcohol, so I guess all the noise is this poor little mite going through withdrawal symptoms. You might have to find a dropper full of alcohol, and then wean him off the alcohol slowly."

As a nurse rushed out to call the doctor, Jackson held the baby, looked at the open, blank eyes, and held the shaking body. When the doctor hurried back into the room, he glowered at Jackson.

"How could you let your wife injure your child by excessively drinking? We'll have to do cognitive tests as we wean him off the alcohol."

Jackson glared at the doctor.

"I thought you blokes were supposed to be smart. Blind Freddy can see that the poor little boy is not my child, and considering I tried everything I could to get her to stop, I feel no guilt, only sorrow for the baby."

Jackson glanced at Marissa. "Don't worry; I'll tell your parents about their new grandson. Considering your father called me a wowser and your mother said a few drinks never hurt anyone, I hope they're prepared to put their money up for the twenty-four-hour, seven-days-a-week care your child will need for the rest of his life."

Jackson entered the waiting room, and Marissa's parents stood to meet him. Jackson hailed a nurse and asked if they could use a private room. Once inside the room, Leo Bossinelli rounded on Jackson.

"What is all the cloak-and-dagger stuff? We want to see our daughter and our grandson."

"Before seeing your daughter, you need to know a few things. The first thing is that your grandson is not my child. You have blackmailed me to stay with your daughter for nearly five months, and even though I told you she fucked everything with a pulse, I had to put my life on hold until she produced a black baby. Considering the number of men who have bedded your daughter, she probably doesn't even know who the father is."

Jackson felt no guilt when Leo sank into a chair, and Maria let out a strangled cry.

"Do you remember when I came to you to beg you to stop Marissa drinking? You called me a wowser, and Maria said a few drinks didn't hurt anyone. Your grandson is in the nursery where they are feeding him a dropper of brandy because he is suffering from withdrawal, seeing as Marissa couldn't drink in the delivery room. By his glazed eyes, I suspect there is brain damage. Leo, I can play the blackmail game too. Unless you expedite my divorce from your daughter, I will offer an interview to a television show and give the rights to the story of Marissa and my marriage to a scandal rag. I will spill all the details and clarify to everyone that you two are as much to blame for the baby's condition as your daughter is. I will release the story if I hear negative comments about myself or my businesses. You have put my life on hold, and I don't want to wait another minute to get rid of the lot of you."

Leo ran a hand over his face. Had he been anyone else, Jackson would have felt sympathy for the cluster fuck surrounding their daughter. Still, after being pulled through the wringer by the Bossinelli family, Jackson couldn't find a shred of empathy.

Chapter Twenty-Eight

Shannon had relented and joined her family for a meal at the pub. She wasn't sure what was happening with Jax and the Bossinelli family, but the longer it took for Jax to ring her, the more concerned she became. How long did it take to apply for custody of a child? If Marissa or her parents challenged the process, Jax could be tied up for months before the issue was resolved. With her mind distracted by thoughts of Jax, it took Shannon a moment or two to focus on the conversation that was doing the rounds of the table. Who was selling their house? Her mother said, " It is the best solution, Shannon. Once you and Andrew live together, you won't need the place you bought near the university."

Shannon blinked. Was her family giving her instructions on how she should live the rest of her life? When the phone rang, she answered it, relieved to escape the ridiculous conversation between her parents and Andrew.

"Shann, sweetheart, I'm outside the door. Can you meet me?"

"Are you free?"

"Yes."

"Come inside; you need to meet my family."

"Okay."

Shannon squealed with joy as she raced towards the entrance, and when Jax stepped through, she launched herself at him. He staggered and then righted himself as he laughed at her welcome.

"Oh, my God. Oh my God, you're here. I was beginning to wonder what the hold-up was."

"There were things I had to do, but we can talk after I meet your family. But first..."

Jackson cupped her face and kissed her, dissolving all the pent-up emotions he had put on hold while pandering to Marissa. When Jax pulled away, Shannon put her head on his chest. Jax wrapped his arms around her, and she gave a contented sigh as she listened to the steady beat of his heart.

"I love you."

"I love you, too. Now that we're both free, I intend to say that daily. Let's meet your parents, and then I want your undivided attention for the next ten days. Wait a moment. Give me your hand."

Jax removed the promise ring from Shannon's right hand and slid it on her ring finger.

"This ring will have to do for now, but I will buy you another ring when I propose."

Shannon and Jax walked towards her family, and the variety of expressions amused her; her brother and sister-in-law looked pleased to see Shannon so obviously in love, but her parents and Andrew looked aghast. The only family member who looked unimpressed was her sister Camille.

"Mum and Dad, I'd like you to meet my fiancé, Jackson Caruthers. Jax, I'd like you to meet my parents, Paul and Kathy."

Good manners prompted her father to offer his hand, but her mother remained seated, her face expressionless, and didn't raise a smile. When Shannon introduced Jax to her sister, brother and sister-in-law, they responded with smiles and handshakes.

"What about an introduction to me?"

Shannon grimaced before turning to Jax. "This is my ex-husband, Andrew, who won't take the hint and get lost."

Shannon tucked her hand through Jax's arm and said,

"Jackson and I have lots of catching up, so we'll see you later."

"Wait, you can't leave, Shannon. You have to marry Andrew, or we will be financially ruined."

Shannon turned back to her mother and noticed she was wringing her hands, and tears welled in her eyes. Jax raised his eyebrows at Shannon and guided her back to the table.

"Mrs Westcott, Shannon will not marry that cad Andrew, regardless of the supposed consequences. Maybe you would like to explain your financial situation and how Shannon marrying Andrew would help."

Kathy Westcott looked at her husband, and he sighed.

Paul Westcott said, "After Shannon and Andrew broke up, Andrew had a lot of financial pressures."

"We didn't break up; Andrew dumped me for another woman."

"Shann, let your Dad explain; even though you want to rip this bloke's throat out, we need to know what we're up against."

"When Andrew's lady friend left, he had bills for their rental property and utility bills to pay, but his finances were low because his friend had wanted a high-class living experience, and Andrew fell into debt trying to accommodate her. We offered our spare room for him; we couldn't see him homeless because he was like a son to us."

Shannon watched her former husband with incredulity. How could he have squandered his nest egg and the proceeds of the house in such a short time? Jax squeezed her hand, and she watched as her family found the words for the rest of the story.

Kathy Westcott said, "Andrew had a friend in real estate, and he had the first offer on a block of land that developers wanted to turn into an upmarket housing estate. The permits were approved, and when the friend offered to include Andrew, he came to us to help finance the deal. We mortgaged the house, and Andrew used the money to fund the investment. However, COVID-19 emerged, and the developer withdrew from the agreement. The developer did not refund the money because he had used it on permits and infrastructure. We put the repayments to the bank on quarterly repayments, but the money is due in a few weeks, and we can't afford to pay."

"How does my marrying Andrew help the situation?"

"Goodness, Shannon, are you so dense? If you move in with Andrew, you can sell your place near the university, and then, because Andrew is your husband, he could pay you back with the proceeds of the house."

"So Andrew gets to screw me over a second time. It's not happening. I can't believe you let Andrew talk you into risking your life savings and the house. I will sell the house, but believe me, I will resent losing my home again because of Andrew."

"Wait, Shann. You don't have to do that." Before Jackson could finish his comment, Andrew cut in.

"Mind your own business, Caruthers. You can't come here in your designer suit, throwing your weight around."

Jackson glared at Andrew and said, "It seems you are the last person who needs to speak. I have a suggestion to prevent Shannon from being forced to sell her house."

Jax quirked his eyebrows at Paul Westcott, and when the man nodded, he laid out his plan.

"I will pay the due bill, but there are some conditions. Are you interested?"

"Yes, we are."

Kathy Westcott wasn't such an easy sell. "We don't know what the conditions are. If Shannon sells her house, we can pay the bill in full; it's much easier."

"Mrs Westcott, I'm stunned at how easily you are willing to sacrifice Shannon's assets. I know you have pressured Shanon to forgive that cheat and remarry him to bail you out of a debt you willingly undertook. Now, do you want help? I will strongly urge Shannon not to sell her house. What happens when Shannon pays the debt, and wonder-boy there comes up with another sure-fire winner?"

Chris, Shannon's brother, had remained silent during the revelation of his parents' financial problem, but couldn't stay quiet any longer.

"Mum and Dad, Tammy and I have sat here week after week as you hassled Shannon to reunite with Andrew. The man left Shannon. He left her to sort out the finances and the other things associated with a marriage breakdown. Shannon worked for weeks wrapping up their affairs, and Andrew refused to talk to her; she had to contact him through his lawyer. You said Andrew would come to his senses from the beginning, and that Shannon should forgive this mistake. The damned man didn't make a mistake. He treated Shannon like a navvy for their entire marriage, disrespected her daily and then cheated. Andrew didn't make a mistake. He broke his wedding vows, and when the other chick ditched him, he came crawling back. If Jax can sort out how to pay your bill, you should get down on your knees and thank him. Selling Shannon's major asset to cover an account you foolishly accrued is not what good parents do."

The people at the table remained silent until Paul Westcott said, "You're right, Chris. We got into this mess and shouldn't expect Shannon to bail us out. Jackson, we would be grateful for your assistance and look forward to your conditions."

Jax looked at Shannon and grinned. "It seems we need to sort out your parents' problem before we discuss our future."

Shannon cupped his face and brushed her lips across his. She felt him shiver, and a smile crossed her face.

"I have waited endless months for you, my love, so that a few more hours won't matter."

Chapter Twenty-Nine

Jackson grabbed a napkin and pulled a pen from the inside pocket of his jacket.

"If I jot down my conditions here, you can discuss them later if you like, but be assured that we won't have a deal if you disagree. The first condition is that you must evict Andrew. Unless I'm mistaken, he has a well-paid job to afford the rent on a house or unit."

Andrew looked aghast.

"I have too many debts to pay to afford rent."

"Mate, contact a debtors agency where they can sort out your debts and work with your creditors to make a payment plan. Your lousy financial situation is your fault, so man up and take responsibility for your actions."

Jax continued. "The second condition is that instead of subsidising your daughter's lifestyle, you charge her rent or move her out."

Kathy Westcott gasped, and Camille glared at Jax.

Kathy spoke first. "You want us to stop supporting our daughter? What kind of parents do you think we are?'

"In truth, Mrs Westcott, you are foolish parents. I assume your daughter has a room at your house, eats your food, uses your electricity and water and generally has an easy life. What does she get paid? Looking at her tonight, I see she is wearing designer jeans and a shirt, and her bag is top-of-the-line. I can't see her shoes from where I sit, but I'll bet they cost a bomb. If you charge her $200 a week in rent, that money could go a long way toward covering your day-to-day expenses.

Even if you resent what I'm saying, surely you realise you can't afford to subsidise your daughter's lavish lifestyle forever?"

Paul Westcott nodded. "You are saying what I've been thinking for a long time. What is your next condition?"

"Once I pay the first payment, we will meet with the bank and get a payout figure. If you've complied with my conditions, I will pay the mortgage, but I will keep the mortgage documents so that Andrew can't entice you to try any more get-rich-quick schemes that your deadbeat ex-son-in-law devises."

Paul Westcott looked at Shannon. "You know this man well; can we trust him with the mortgage documents?"

Shannon smiled at her father. "Jackson Caruthers is one of the most honourable men I know. While you may not know what kept us apart for so long, I can tell you that he was trying to fulfil his obligations. Your mortgage documents will be safe with Jackson."

Jax stood and drew Shannon to her feet. "Mr Westcott, if you or your wife have any questions, please don't hesitate to ask. I will contact you in a day or two to organise the loan repayment, but Shannon and I have much catching up to do right now."

As Shannon and Jax walked away, Jax asked, "Do you want food or to talk first?"

Shannon smiled. "I can walk and chew gum, so let's do both."

Jax laughed. "God, I've missed your quirky sense of humour and kind heart, but most of all, I've missed your kisses and presence in my bed. Let's do both."

Once they arrived at the hotel, the lure of food was not strong enough to prevent them from falling into bed. It had been months since they shared a bed, and Shannon knew it would take many months before the urgency to make love would dim. Eventually, sated and exhausted, Shannon raised the question of food again, and this time, Jax agreed. As he rang for room service, Shannon cleaned up in the bathroom. The smell of food drew her away from her ablutions, and she joined Jax as he sat on the ground with the food spread around him. Shannon grinned at her executive lover sitting cross-legged on the carpet. When she joined him, she piled a large amount of food on her plate and began devouring the delicious spread the hotel provided. Sometime later, she pushed her empty plate away from her and said, "Jackson, my love, I want answers."

Jax nodded, but before he launched into an explanation, he poured each of them a glass of wine. His narration of their time apart took a while, and when it culminated in the baby's birth, Shannon groaned.

"So this baby will spend a lifetime filled with avoidable challenges. I can't believe Marissa's parents were oblivious to her lifestyle and angry that they didn't release you sooner or listen to your concerns regarding the baby's health. But once the baby was born, you didn't contact me or visit for another six weeks."

"I wasn't game enough to leave Perth until the divorce came through because Leo Bossinelli is a slimy character, and if he could find a way to silence me while still ruining my businesses, he would have. Let's pack the leftovers on the trolley, and I'll park it outside; I need to discuss something with you."

Shannon slid onto the bed, her back propped against the bedhead, watching Jax maneuver the trolley through the door. He was so handsome it almost hurt to look at him, but Shannon was confident that the sight of her sexy boyfriend would never grow old. Jax slid onto the bed next to her and, grasping her hands in his, said, "Shann, I know it is our destiny to be together, but we have a problem with distance. I can't return to seeing you once a month when I want to wake up next to you. Would you move to the West with me? There would be opportunities in the hospitals there for physiotherapists, so you needn't give up your job."

"Jax, I need only one thing in Western Australia: you. I'm done with my family and would be willing to move to Perth, Albany, or wherever you set up your home base. My family has proven to be unsupportive and self-serving throughout our entire relationship, and while I'll miss Chris and Tammy, I'll be glad to be rid of the rest. It seems that Andrew will never get the message and stop thinking we can reunite, and even though you have forced my parents to move him out of the house, I believe he will continue to attend family functions."

"Thank God, I didn't want to move to Melbourne, but if that were the only option, I would have moved."

"There is one thing I haven't told you. I'm not employed at a hospital, but have been working in aged care since the visit you and that bitch made so she could distribute her father's wealth. Your darling wife black-banned me, and she told them any hospital or clinic that hoped to secure funding would be ineligible if I were employed there."

Jax growled."Shit! I must say I knew she was a cow, but what weak-kneed people the hospital admin is to allow her to call the shots. Bring your resume with you, and I will tell Leo Bossinelli if his bitch of a daughter does anything to besmirch your reputation, I will ruin her."

Shannon laughed. " As it turned out, she did me a good turn. The aged care sector is woefully underfunded, and most residents sit in front of the telly waiting to die. With my supervisor's approval, I developed a program that got people away from the telly and back into worthwhile tasks. I can show you later, but I've placed a copywrite on my program and sent DVDs and written transcripts to other centres. The improvement in residents' health and well-being following the program's initiation is impressive. I'd love to see it implemented Australia-wide."

Jax laughed. "You're like that fairytale where the girl had to spin straw into gold."

When he wrapped his arms around Shannon, they became so spellbound by each other that jobs and location took a back seat to love and passion.

Epilogue

As Shannon and Jax entered his parents' house, the noise level rose tenfold as his family hugged them and asked a million questions. Shannon loved these people; they accepted her even after last year's turmoil, and the welcome was heartening after her parents dismissed her feelings. Jackson's mother, Margie, was the first to see the engagement ring, and she burst into tears. For a moment, Shannon stood motionless, fearing that her future mother-in-law was distraught, until Margie said, "Happy tears, Shannon, they are happy tears."

Shannon let out a sigh of relief. "Thank goodness, even though this bloke is worth waiting almost a year for, I didn't want to battle his mother for him."

Everyone crowded around to admire the ring.

Once everyone finished with their greetings, they moved to the kitchen, where an assortment of cakes and biscuits covered the table.

"When is the wedding?" Jax's mother asked.

"And where is the wedding being held?" his sister interrupted.

Jax answered the questions. "We've waited long enough, so the wedding will be as soon as we can get it organised. Mum, can you and Dana help Shannon with the wedding planning? I'll give opinions, but the stuff women want is all a mystery." With a grin at Shannon, he said, "Will choosing my groomsmen's suits and arriving at the venue on time be okay?"

Shannon laughed. "As long as you are there when I arrive, I will be a happy woman. Oh, and the wedding will be in whatever venue we can secure in Albany."

Jax added, "Shannon is moving to Albany soon, and we will make our home here."

Bert Caruthers, who had remained quiet until Jax revealed Shannon's move, said,

"Shannon, are you close to your parents? Will you miss them?"

"Bert, the answer is no, I'm not close and won't miss them. To be truthful, I'm glad to be away from them. While Jax battled with the Bossinellis, I fought with my family. They kept trying to pressure me into reuniting with my controlling, cheating ex-husband. Before we left Melbourne, we discovered my ex had talked my parents into investing in a property development that went bust. That would be upsetting at the best of times, but they had mortgaged the house to loan him the money, and they thought that if I moved back in with him, I could sell the house I had bought from the division of funds after the divorce and secure their mortgage. Thank goodness Jax sorted out the mess, but they are no longer my favourite people. I will miss my brother and his wife, but I hope to entice them to take a holiday here."

Margie frowned and said, "I'm sorry to hear that. Why is your ex still in contact with your parents if he deserted you? Shouldn't they be angry about the way he treated you? We will never welcome Marissa or her family to any of our events. After what she did to Jackson, she is public enemy number one, and your ex put you through hell. I can't understand your parents' attitude."

"I appreciate your understanding. You would think my parents would support me, but my mother insists Andrew is like a son to her. I once told her that I wasn't her daughter, but if he were her son, she would ignore my anger and continue to include him in all our social outings. More than once, I confided in my family about the state of my marriage, and my parents seemed to think the relationship was salvageable. While Jax wasn't on the scene, they thought nothing would come from our relationship, even though I assured them we'd be together when he sorted out his life."

Late that evening, Shannon felt emotionally and physically drained. They had filled the day with talking, laughing, and so much food that Shannon thought she might burst. Before they left, Margie, Dana and Shannon set a date to begin the wedding preparations. This time, she had no doubts that Jax's involvement in the wedding preparations would be as he stated, and it was nice to have his sister and mother to help with the arrangements.

Weeks later, Paul Wetscott scrutinised Shannon's face as he prepared to walk her down the aisle for the second time.

"I don't remember you being so excited when you married Andrew."

"Dad, after the controlling way Andrew acted when we were planning the wedding, I had reservations, but I put it down to last-minute nerves. Even at the beginning of our relationship, I never felt for Andrew what I did for Jax. Being apart for so long was torture, and it convinced me that he was my life partner."

"I'm sorry your mother and I tried to convince you to reunite with Andrew. In the beginning, it was because we thought you were throwing away a good relationship because of his infidelity, but when the deal went poorly and we lost our money, we were desperate to find a way to pay our mortgage. It was selfish of us, and I'm sorry. I hope this bloke makes you happy."

Shannon beamed. "I have no doubts that we will have differences of opinion, but after the adversity we have endured, being together is a gift neither of us will ever take for granted."

When the music began, Shannon walked along the aisle to the man who started as a one-night stand and, after an unexpected romance, would be her forever love.

Also by Robyn C Rye

Farnsworth Sisters
Marrying a Rogue
Rescuing Hannah

The Buckingham Sisters
Lady Maggie's Challenge
Layla's Unwanted Husband

The Evans Family
Sometimes Love is not Enough
Still the One
Moving Forward

Standalone
One More Chance
Lady Jayne's Reputation
Third Time's the Charm
Can't Stop Loving You

The Marriage Scam
An Unlikely Match
Searching For You
The Unexpected Suitor
The Lady and the Duke
Starting Over
An Unforgettable Stranger
The Duke's Revenge
The Temporary Wife
Against The Odds
Betrayed
No Good Turn Goes Unpunished
Lady Eloise's Soldier
Lillian's Forbidden Beau
Remember Me
Always Second Best
When One Door Closes
Coming Home to You
Chasing Shadows
Fool Me Once
Deserting Lady Audrey
My Unlikely Saviour
Lies and Deception
A New Beginning
Julia's Second Chance
The Hidden Enemy
The Maiden's Redemption
Miss Elizabeth's Season